SIMPLE'S UNCLE SAM

Simple's Uncle Sam

LANGSTON HUGHES

Hill and Wang
A division of Farrar, Straus and Giroux
New York

Hill and Wang
A division of Farrar, Straus and Giroux
18 West 18th Street, New York 10011

Copyright © 1965 by Langston Hughes,
renewed 1993 by Arnold Rampersad and Ramona Bass
Introduction copyright © 2000 by Akiba Sullivan Harper
All rights reserved
Distributed in Canada by Douglas & McIntyre Ltd.
Printed in the United States of America
First published in 1965 by Hill and Wang
First paperback edition, 1965
Revised edition, 2000

Library of Congress Cataloging-in-Publication Data
Hughes, Langston, 1902–1967.
    Simple's Uncle Sam / Langston Hughes. — Rev. ed.
       p.   cm.
    ISBN 0-8090-8681-6 (pbk.)
    1. Simple (Fictitious character)—Fiction.   2. Afro-American men—
Fiction.   3. Afro-Americans—Fiction.   4. Humorous stories, American.
I. Title.
PS3515.U274 S6   2000
813'.52—dc21   99-057066

10   9   8   7   6   5   4

www.fsgbooks.com

To my long-time friends,
Henri and Eli Cartier-Bresson

The author thanks the Associated
Negro Press International, the *New York Post*,
the *Chicago Defender*, and the *Saturday Review* for
permission to reprint these Simple stories.

CONTENTS

INTRODUCTION

Langston Hughes enjoys a solid reputation in both popular and scholarly circles of literature. Without a doubt, he deserves his fame as a poet, and he clearly played a crucial role during the celebrated Harlem Renaissance. Nevertheless, Hughes continued writing far beyond anyone's definition of the Renaissance period, and in nearly every conceivable genre. Like his poetry, Hughes's works in theater, children's literature, folklore, autobiography, and short fiction have garnered critical attention and popularity. In short fiction, none of his characters captured the hearts and minds of readers as did Jesse B. Semple, better known as Simple.

Langston Hughes was already established as a poet of the people when he began a column in the *Chicago Defender* in 1942. The weekly newspaper was one of the most popular African American papers in the nation, and World War II carried it around the world. In an effort to help his audience share his own view of global events, in 1943 Hughes created Jesse B. Semple to express the views of ordinary black men. Through Simple, Hughes strove to eradicate parochial thinking and to help all his readers appreciate why they needed to overlook temporarily the racial segregation of the U.S. armed services in order to combat Hitler—a greater and more immediate force of evil than Jim Crow. Hughes soon learned that Simple struck a familiar note with the readers of the *Defender*. Fans celebrated Simple's voice, advised him about women, and even sent gifts to Simple and his lady friends.

The character developed into the dominant voice in many of Hughes's columns through the 1940s. Hughes's editorial wisdom shrank to a mostly anonymous foil. Increasingly, he spoke through Simple. This was not a departure for Hughes, for in his poetry he had demonstrated a gift for capturing the voices of many speakers, very much in the tradition of Walt Whitman or Paul Laurence Dunbar. His first volume of short stories, *The Ways of White Folks*, had pointed out the puzzling behaviors of whites. His social commentaries had revealed the foolish cruelties of American capitalism, at home and abroad. And Hughes had sought from his youth to make a living for himself as a writer, a writer who could reach audiences of many races both during and beyond the age of the creation of his works.

The Simple stories gave Hughes his first assurance of a black audience, thereby allowing him to address his favorite topics to his favorite audience. Yet Hughes labored for years to craft Simple into a character who could touch readers beyond the black press. He captured that wider audience when he published the columns in book form—*Simple Speaks His Mind* (1950), *Simple Takes a Wife* (1953), and *Simple Stakes a Claim* (1957). Hughes also used the columns as the basis of his 1957 musical, *Simply Heavenly*. Although the musical is occasionally revived, regrettably all three of the early story collections have gone out of print. Most contemporary readers know Simple from Hughes's omnibus collection, *The Best of Simple*

(1961), and from the edited collection *The Return of Simple* (1994), which incorporates material from the out-of-print books. With this revival of *Simple's Uncle Sam* (1965), Hughes's last volume of stories, readers have an opportunity to examine Simple within a more restricted time period and to see him interact with topical events more faithfully than he does in the broader collections.

The episodes in *Simple's Uncle Sam* are probably the least known of all the Simple episodes. It is the only one of Hughes's own collections to appear after *The Best of Simple*, and Hughes boasted that none of the episodes had appeared in book form before. Perhaps more important, many of these episodes were originally published in the *New York Post*, where Hughes's weekly column moved after he had reached an impasse with the *Chicago Defender* over financial arrangements in 1962. While the *Defender* had provided a friendly, mostly black, and very empathetic audience familiar with Hughes's many literary accomplishments, the *Post* gave Hughes readers less familiar with the life and views of Simple. In fact, readers of the *Post* were often unfamiliar with Hughes himself.

From his replies to fan mail, we can conclude that Hughes had to explain a great deal to his *Post* readers—not only his own views but also the language, imagery, and allusions of Simple. Outrage about congressional lethargy or about mysterious Southern lynchings drew complaints from *Post* readers who wondered why Hughes never mentioned the Holocaust or other atrocities inflicted upon groups other than blacks. Other *Post* readers were angry young blacks who felt that Simple's vernacular black English and his frequent use of humor signaled an offensive and intolerable "Uncle Tom" attitude. Archival materials may not preserve all the fan mail from either audience,

but, judging by what is housed in Yale University's Bei-
necke Library and New York City's Schomburg Center, we
have to wonder if the faithful and devoted fans who followed Simple in the *Defender* missed the switch to the
Post. Perhaps Hughes saved only those letters that focused
on the friction and minimized the kudos. Or perhaps the
times had become so volatile that readers of any publica-
tion would have bristled at Simple's parochial viewpoints,
grammatical errors, and penchant to laugh whenever possible. Contemporary readers can evaluate *Simple's Uncle
Sam* from a safe historical distance in a different political
climate.

Simple's Uncle Sam continues Hughes's tradition of pre-
senting Simple's blunt assessments of the U.S. government, barbs about women, revenge fantasies about white
racists, and challenges to hypocrisy. Unlike *Simple Takes a
Wife*, this collection does not provide sequential episodes
about Simple's personal life. More like *Simple Stakes a
Claim*, *Simple's Uncle Sam* always keeps one foot in the
political realm and pivots from that point.

Politically, Simple emerges somewhere between Martin
Luther King, Jr., and Malcolm X. He recognizes and respects the accomplishments of nonviolence but also shares
some of Malcolm's disdain for all the sit-ins and marches.
Declaring his own vision, Simple suggests that African
American nude pose-outs (or pose-ins, for those who work
inside) could accomplish more than conventional nonviolent strategies "to shock America into clothing us in the
garments of equality, not the rags of segregation." However, Simple also has moments when he advocates and fan-
tasizes about violence: "Rev. Martin Luther King tries to
pray prejudice out, but sometimes I think we are gonna
have to flay it out." He goes on to speculate about what

might happen to the Negro's right to vote in Mississippi "if all them down-home colored folks was to rise up in one mass, imagine!"

Simple's proclivity to challenge racists reflects his own migration from Virginia to Harlem, a history detailed in earlier collections but only alluded to in *Simple's Uncle Sam*. Having grown up in the South, Simple experienced firsthand both subtle and brutal manifestations of racism. Yet, having migrated first to Baltimore and finally to Harlem, Simple learned how to stretch his opportunities. Simple understands what is considered normal in the South, but he also holds that norm in contempt. Unlike blacks who remained in the South, Simple enjoys a bolder, brasher relationship with police officers and political officials. Indeed, Simple boasts about his own representative to Congress, Adam Clayton Powell, Jr., and engages his white boss in toe-to-toe debate about the needs and wants of Negroes, refusing to allow his boss to determine what THE Negro wants. In his dreams and fantasies, Simple reconstructs the South, reversing racial barriers, hierarchies, and financial power structures. Yet, by his own admission, Simple refuses to return to the South to tackle the actual dangerous work of Freedom Rides and voter registration drives.

In addition to questioning grim political realities, Simple expounds on social mores when he casts an eye on the women in his world. He dwells upon Joyce, his wife, who thrives on pretentious cultural events and aspires to budget their two salaries so that they can afford to buy a home in the suburbs. His domestic tranquillity is frequently shaken by his needy Cousin Minnie, who enjoys bars as much as Simple does. Another cousin, Lynn Clarisse, shares Simple's Southern roots but is college-educated, financially secure, and culturally open-minded. Unlike any other character in the entire canon, Lynn Clarisse is a proud Freedom Rider and an active worker in the voter registration drives. Her visit to Harlem is truly understood to be a visit, because her commitment rests with her activities back home.

Contemporary readers can justifiably label Simple a sexist, as he boldly expresses many offensive and restrictive views about women. He portrays his former wife, Isabel, and his cousin Minnie as gold diggers and usurpers. He expects Joyce to have his dinner on the table each night, despite her own employment outside the home. Simple even wants to hold an "Ugly Contest" every weekend, because he finds "more homely womens in the world than there are pretty womens." The total scope of the volume, however, shatters any monolithic image of black women. Joyce adores opera. Lynn Clarisse reverts to the words of Sartre in times of stress. Even Cousin Minnie becomes boldly active during the 1964 Harlem riots, and she takes a courageous stand against physical abuse in a personal relationship. These women represent a range of female viewpoints, preferences, and activities. Moreover, Simple's sexist point of view is usually countered by his constant companion and beer buddy, Mr. Boyd.

Boyd, usually the unnamed "I" with whom Simple dialogues, is actually named in several of the episodes in *Simple's Uncle Sam.* This financially secure fellow frequents the same bar as Simple. The other patrons value his college education, but Boyd never flaunts it or uses it to lord over his companions. He challenges Simple's sobriety, his sanity, and his sense, but his role in these stories is always as a foil to Simple. Although Boyd challenges Simple's focus on race, Simple generally gains the upper hand or the last laugh. These two characters were developed to be dramatically different, but together they represent the kind of mutual respect for diverse socio-economic factors that characterized Langston Hughes himself. Their combined attitudes epitomize the behaviors and perspectives Hughes wanted his Simple stories to advance.

While Simple dominates nearly every episode, the occasional story is carried by another character: Boyd, Cousin Minnie, or the deeply racist Colonel Cushenberry, who offers his "Cracker Prayer" as he nears death. Hughes pays careful attention to distinctions in dialect, diction, grammar, and opinions, and by doing so conveys an important multiplicity of voices. Thus, what appears to be uncomplicated nonetheless functions in profound ways to challenge the status quo and suggest possibilities for change. As the beer buddy Boyd says, "Simplicity can sometimes be more devious than erudition."

As in the weekly newspaper columns, the episodes in *Simple's Uncle Sam* burst with references to real people, creating a graceful blend of fiction and historical footage. Comedians such as Moms Mabley, Pigmeat Markham, and Nipsey Russell, and athletes such as Cassius Clay (Muhummad Ali), Willie Mays, Casey Stengel, Jackie Robinson, and Wilt Chamberlain became part of the literary landscape. Opera singers such as Leontyne Price and Marian Anderson are mentioned, along with the pop performers Billy Eckstine, Harry Belafonte, and Frank Sinatra, and the gospel artists James Cleveland and the Dixie Hummingbirds. Actors including Nina Mae McKinney, Sidney Poitier, Claudia McNeil, and Elizabeth Taylor all cross the stage, and works by Shakespeare and LeRoi Jones (Amiri Baraka) are cited. Literature by Whitman

and Sartre, operas by Wagner and Bizet, and artistic mas-
terpieces such as the Venus de Milo and the Mona Lisa
become part of the environment. Simple frequently men-
tions Harlem's Congressman, Adam Clayton Powell, Jr.,
along with presidents from Franklin D. Roosevelt to Lyn-
don B. Johnson. African American organizations such as
the Urban League emerge as forces of change. Indelible
events such as the bombing deaths of four little girls in a
Birmingham Sunday School, the lynching of Emmitt Till,
and the murder of Medgar Evers become salient references.

These political and historical realities are planted in a
field blooming with humor—coined words, laughable character names, and malapropisms. Who can resist a chuckle
when Cousin Minnie confronts her inebriated date Rombow and "conk[s] and crown[s him] both all at once," or
when Simple recalls wondering in Sunday School what
kind of drawers Jesus wore beneath his flowing garments?
Even the ironic characters in Simple's dreams, like "dear
old Mammy Faubus," "Mammy Eastland," and the "little
blue-eyed crackerninnies," amuse those who recognize the
deeply entrenched racism those names represent.

Simple's flights of fantasy sometimes give him power
and wealth. The boat whistle on his imaginary yacht would
blow in B-flat, "the key of the blues." In his imagined
heaven, Simple threatens those who would impose racial
barriers at the golden gate: "If you and Old Gov. there
don't get out of my way and let me in this gate, I will take
my left wing and slap you both down." When Simple lauds
the Europeans for dropping race barriers in restaurants,
hospitals, and cemeteries, he concludes, "They has no such
jackassery in Europe." Just when the reader might have
grown too weary of the litany of problems, Simple invents

a word to lighten the moment. Situational humor, verbal incongruities, and satire all diffuse the hostility resulting from truly offensive racial restrictions.

Humor aside, *Simple's Uncle Sam* also provides the poignant, timeless, and thought-provoking moments for which Hughes is better known in other genres. For example, Cousin Minnie's heartbreaking experience with her man leads Simple to note, "Some people do not have no scars on their faces, . . . but they has scars on their hearts." Simple, like Hughes himself, observes the inner workings of people. Many of Simple's fantasies of generosity echo the sentiments and actions of his creator. Whereas Simple wishes to buy a bicycle for every youth in Harlem, Hughes allowed the children to his neighborhood to "garden" in the tiny plot of dirt in front of his brownstone.

For those who may have grown numb reviewing the familiar "I have a dream" speech of King and the "by any means necessary" speech of Malcolm, *Simple's Uncle Sam* provides a fresh opportunity to consider and appreciate the opinions of an ordinary person in the midst of oppressive forces. Whether he discusses poignant realities or outrageous fantasies, Jesse B. Semple weaves a web that sticks. With this revival of *Simple's Uncle Sam*, the reading public can rediscover a vital chapter in America's history.

AKIBA SULLIVAN HARPER
Spelman College

SIMPLE'S UNCLE SAM

CENSUS

"I have had so many hardships in this life," said Simple, "that it is a wonder I'll live until I die. I was born young, black, voteless, poor, and hungry, in a state where white folks did not even put Negroes on the census. My daddy said he were never counted in his life by the United States government. And nobody could find a birth certificate for me nowhere. It were not until I come to Harlem that one day a census taker dropped around to my house and asked me where were I born and why, also my age and if I was still living. I said, 'Yes, I am here, in spite of all.'

" 'All of what?' asked the census taker. 'Give me the data.'

" 'All my corns and bunions, for one,' I said. 'I were borned with corns. Most colored peoples get corns so young, they must be inherited. As for bunions, they seem to come natural, we stands on our feet so much. These feet of mine have stood in everything from soup lines to the draft board. They have supported everything from a packing trunk to a hongry woman. My feet have walked ten thousand miles running errands for white folks and another ten thousand trying to keep up with colored. My feet have stood before altars, at crap tables, bars, graves, kitchen doors, welfare windows, and social security railings. Be sure and include my feet on that census you are taking,' I told that man.

"Then I went on to tell him how my feet have helped to keep the American shoe industry going, due to the money I have spent on my feet. 'I have wore out seven hundred pairs of shoes, eighty-nine tennis shoes, forty-four summer sandals, and two hundred and two loafers. The socks my feet have bought could build a knitting mill. The razor blades I have used cutting away my corns could pay for a razor plant. Oh, my feet have helped to make America rich, and I am still standing on them.

" 'I stepped on a rusty nail once, and mighty near had lockjaw. And from my feet up, so many other things have happened to me, since, it is a wonder I made it through this world. In my time, I have been cut, stabbed, run over, hit by a car, tromped by a horse, robbed, fooled, deceived, double-crossed, dealt seconds, and mighty near black-mailed—but I am still here! I have been laid off, fired and not rehired, Jim Crowed, segregated, insulted, eliminated, locked in, locked out, locked up, left holding the bag, and denied relief. I have been caught in the rain, caught in jails, caught short with my rent, and caught with the wrong woman—but I am still here!

" 'My mama should have named me Job instead of Jesse B. Semple. I have been underfed, underpaid, undernourished, and everything but undertaken—yet I am still here. The only thing I am afraid of now—is that I will die before my time. So man, put me on your census now this year, because I may not be here when the next census comes around.'

"The census man said, 'What do you expect to die of—complaining?'

" 'No,' I said, 'I expect to ugly away.' At which I thought the man would laugh. Instead you know he nodded his head, and wrote it down. He were white and did not know I was making a joke. Do you reckon that man really thought I am homely?"

SWINGING HIGH

"A meat ball by any other name is still a meat ball just the same," said Simple. "My wife, Joyce, is a fiend for foreign foods. Almost every time she drags me downtown to a show, she wants to go eat in some new kind of restaurant, Spanish, French, Greek, or who knows what? Last night we had something writ on the menu in a Philippine restaurant in big letters as BOLA-BOLAS. They returned out to be nothing but meat balls."

"*Bola* probably means 'ball' in their language," I said. "But I am like Joyce. I sort of go for foreign foods, too—something different once in a while, you know."

"Me, I like plain old down-home victuals, soul food with corn bread," said Simple, "spare ribs, pork chops, and things like that. Ham hock, string beans, salt pork and cabbage."

"All good foods," I said, "but for a change, why not try chicken curry and rootie next time you take Joyce out."

"What is that?" asked Simple.

"An East Indian dish, chicken stewed in curry sauce."

"I am not West Indian nor East," said Simple.

"You don't have to be foreign to like foreign food," I said.

"Left to me, I would go to Jenny Lou's up yonder on

(4)

Seventh Avenue across from Small's Paradise. Jenny Lou's is where all the down-home folks eat when they is visiting Harlem. They knows good home-like food a mile away by the way it smells."

"A restaurant is not supposed to smell," I said. "The scent of cooking is supposed to be kept in the kitchen."

"Jenny Lou's kitchen is in the dining room," said Simple. "When I were a single man, I et there often. Them low prices suited my pocket."

"How about Frank's?" I asked. "Now Negro-owned."

"That's where Joyce takes her society friends like Mrs. Maxwell-Reeves," said Simple. "The menu is as big as newspaper. So many things on it, it is hard to know what to pick out. I like to just say 'pork chops' and be done with it. I don't want soup, neither salad. And who wants rice pudding for dessert? Leave off them things, also olives. Just give me pork chops."

"Is that all?"

"I'll take the gravy," Simple said.

"Pork chops, bread, and gravy," I shook my head. "As *country* as you can be!"

"If that is what you call *country*," said Simple, "still gimme pork chops. Pork chops and fried apples maybe, if they is on the menu. I love fried apples, and my Uncle Tige had an apple tree in his back yard. When I was a little small boy, I used to set in a rope swing behind my Uncle Tige's house. The swing were attached to that apple tree which were a very old apple tree, and big for an apple tree, and a good tree for a swing for boys and girls. It were nice to set in this swing when I was yet a wee small boy and be pushed by the bigger children because I was still too small for my feet to touch the ground, and I did not know how to pump myself up into the air. Later I could. Later I could stand up in that swing and pump myself way up into the air, almost as high as the limb on which the swing were tied. Oh, I remember very well that swing and that apple tree when I were a child.

"It looks to me life is like a swing," continued Simple. "When young, somebody else must push you because your feet are too short to touch the ground and start the swing in motion. But later you go for yourself. By and by, you can stand up and swing high, swing high, way high up, and you are on your own. How wonderful it is to stand up in the swing, pumping all by yourself! But suppose the rope was to break, the tree limb snap off when you have pumped yourself up so high? Suppose it does? You will be the one to fall, nobody else, just you yourself. Yes, life is like a swing! But in spite of all and everything, it is good to swing. Oh, yes! The swing of life is wonderful, but if you are a colored swinger, you have to have a stout heart, pump hard, and hold tight to get even a few feet above the ground. And be careful that your neighbor next door, white, has not cut your rope, so that just when you are swinging highest, it will break and throw you to the ground. 'Look at that Negro swinging! But he done fell!' they say. But someday we gonna swing right up to the very top of the tree and not fall. Yes, someday we will."

"Integrated, I hope," I said.

"Yes, integrated, I reckon," said Simple. "But some folks is getting so wrapped up in this integration thing, white and colored, that I do believe some of them is going stone-cold crazy. You see how here in New York peoples is talking to themselves on busses and in the subways, whirling around in the middle of the street, mumbling and grumbling all by themselves to nobody on park benches, dumping garbage on bridges, slicing up subway seats with knives and nail files, running out of gas on crowded highways on purpose and liable to get smashed up in traffic jams. Oh, I do not know what has come over the human race—like that nice young white minister in Cleveland laying down *behind* a rolling bulldozer, *not* in front of it—where the driver could see him and maybe stop in time before the man got crushed to death. He were protesting Jim Crow—but sometimes the protest is worse than the Crow."

"That earnest white man, no doubt, was trying to call attention to the urgency of the civil rights," I said. "He wanted to keep the movement on the front pages of the newspapers."

"It has been on the front pages of the newspapers for ten years," said Simple, "and if everybody does not know by now something needs to be done about civil rights, they will never know. After so many Freedom Rides and sit-ins and picketings and head bustings and police dogs and bombings and little children blowed up, and teen-agers in jail by the thousands up to now, and big head-lines across the newspapers, colored and white, why did that good white minister in Cleveland with his glasses on have to lay down *behind* a bulldozer?"

"I gather there are some things you would not do for a cause," I said.

"I would not lay down behind a bulldozer going back-wards. How would my dying help anything—and my wife, Joyce, would be left a widow? It is not that I might be dying in a good cause, but let me die on my own two feet, knowing where, when, and why, and maybe making a speech telling off the world—not in a wreck because somebody has stalled a car whilst traffic is speeding. To me that is crazy! Whoever drives them stalled cars might be smashed up and killed too."

"They would consider themselves martyrs," I said.

"They should not make a martyr out of me in another car who do not even know them," said Simple. "Let me make a martyr out of myself, if I want to, but don't make me one under other peoples' cars. I do not want to be a martyr on nobody else's time. And don't roll no bulldozer over me unless I am standing in front, not behind it when it rolls. If I have got to look death in the face ahead of time, at least let me know who is driving. Also don't take me by surprise before I have paid my next year's dues to the NAACP. Anyhow, a car or a bulldozer is a dangerous thing to fool around with, as is any kind of moving machinery. You remember that old joke about the washer-woman who bent over too far and got both her breasts caught in the wringer? There is such a thing as bending over too far—even to get your clothes clean. Certainly there is plenty of dirty linen in this U.S.A., but I do not advise nobody to get their breast caught in a wringer. Machines do not have no sense."

"A cynic might say the same thing about martyrs," I said. "Except sometimes it takes an awful lot of sense to have no sense."

"Maybe you are right," said Simple, "just like it takes a mighty lot of pumping to swing high in the swing of life."

CONTEST

"They are always holding Beauty Contests all over America," said Simple. "Why don't nobody ever hold an Ugly Contest?"

"An Ugly Contest!" I cried. "For what reason?"

"For the same reasons folks hold a Beauty Contest," said Simple, "for fun. There are so many ugly womens in this world, it would be fun to see which one wins."

"Beauty is as beauty does," I reminded him, "not how it looks."

"Oh, no!" declared Simple. "Beauty is as beauty looks. You can't tell me an ugly chick, be she ever so nice, is going to *look* pretty, not even if she goes to church every day and three times on Sunday. She may look holy, but she cannot look pretty if her mama did not born her so."

"The Lord made everyone in God's image," I said.

"Don't bamboozle me like that," said Simple. "If God is bowlegged, sway-backed, merinery, and buck-toothed, skippy! That I do not believe. But some womens is all of them things—and wear slacks besides. There are more homely womens in the world than there are pretty womens. So it would be easy to hold an Ugly Contest every week-end. And at the end of the year I would have an Elimination Contest for the Ugliest Young Woman on Earth. I bet whoever won that Grand Prize would get all kinds of Hollywood, TV, radio, and movie contracts, not to mention a week at the Apollo."

"The winner might get all those things," I said, "but the poor girl would have a hard time finding a husband after so much 'ugly' publicity."

"With all the money that Ugly Champion would be making, she could not keep the men away from her," said Simple. "Facts is, if I was single, as much loot as the most famous ugly woman in the world would be making, I would marry her myself just to spend some of her cash. Ugly is as ugly does, and if that woman did me good, I would not care what she looked like. Then if she uglied away into paradise, died in due time, and willed me her fortunes, my memories of her would be beautiful. No rich woman can get too ugly to find a husband. Money talks."

"Perish the thought," I said, "that the winner of the Ugly Contest would have to pay a man to marry her. Poor girl! That would be a hollow triumph indeed for all her trophies and her scrolls. But tell me, since Beauty Contests have rules, you know, by which beauty is judged—measurements of busts, waists, hips, and thighs, tint of complexion and tone of hair—what rules would you set up for judging an Ugly Contest?"

"Busts the flattest, hips the barrelest, legs the thinnest, and the rest of it, come what may," said Simple. "Also I would give a prize for the tightest slacks on the biggest haunches, the highest heels on the longest feet, and the hair with the most colors in it. Just a two-tone hair job or a wig would not get nowhere in my contest. I would give a prize to the head of hair with a red streak, a yellow streak, a green streak, and a purple streak in it—and only then if it had an orange horsetail as well. Oh, my ugly woman winner would be a mad Myrtle without a girdle, I'm telling you! She would look like King Kong's daughter plus the niece of Balaam's off-ox. To win my contest, she would have to be a homely heifer, indeed.

"But I would give her a great big prize, then put her under contract for all personal appearances on stage, screen, or at Rockland Palace. I would charge one thousand dollars-a-day commission for the public to look at her—the Homeliest Woman in the Whole World. The Ugly Champion of the Universe! If ever she went up in a spaceship, she would scare the Man in the Moon to death before she had a chance to meet him. Miss Ugly would be so ugly she would be proud of herself, and her mama before her would be proud of her, as would her daddy when he learned how famous his daughter had got to be—pictured endorsing every filter-tipped cigarette, singing commercials for toothpaste, and posing for beer.

"Seriously, I believe I will start such a contest, get me maybe a thousand entries, hire a big hall, Count Basie's Band, and have me an Ugly Parade instead of a Beauty Parade, appoint Nipsey Russell and Jackie Moms Mabley as judges, and take a big pile of money. Besides, such a contest would make me famous, too—as the only man in the world with nerve enough to call a *whole lot* of women ugly! 'Jesse B. Semple, promoter of the Ugly Contest!' And if I found a woman uglier than I am a man, more homely than me, I would give her a special prize myself. A gold beer mug with my picture on it, engraved:

To You From Me
Your Ugly Daddy
Jesse B. Semple
Congratulations

EMPTY HOUSES

"Once when I was a wee small child in Virginia," said Simple, "I was walking down the street one real hot day when a white man patted me on the head and give me a dime.

"He said, 'Looks like you could stand an ice-cream cone,' to which I said, 'Yes, sir.'

"That cone I bought sure was good. I were staying with some of my mother's distant kinsfolks at the time and when I went home and told them I had bought an ice-cream cone they said, 'Where did you get the money?'

"I said, 'A white man give me a dime.'

"They said, 'What was you doing out in the street begging for a dime?'

"I explained to them that I had not begged, but they said, 'Don't lie to me, boy. Nobody is gonna walk up to you and just give you a dime without you asking for it.' So I got a whipping for lying.

"They could not understand that there is some few people in the world who do good without being asked. It were a hot day, I were a little boy, and ice-cream cones are always good. And that man just looked at me and thought I would like one—which I did. That is one reason why I do not hate all white folks today because some white folks will do good without being asked or hauled up before the Supreme Court to have a law promulgated against them.

"Not everybody has to be begged to do good, or sub-peanoed into it. Why, a cat in the bar the other night I hardly knowed offered me a beer, and when I said, 'Man, I'm sorry, but I am kinder short tonight and cannot buy you one back,' he said, 'Aw, forget it!' He bought me the beer anyway.

"Some folks think that everything in life has to balance up, turn out equal. If you buy a man a drink, he has to buy you one back. If you get invited to a party, then you have to give a party, too, and invite whoever invited you. My wife, Joyce, is like that—which makes folks end up having to give parties they do not want to give, and going to a lot of parties to which they do not want to go. Tit for tat—I give you this, you give me that. But me, I am not that way. If I was to give somebody I liked a million dollars, I would not expect them to give me a million dollars back. I would give a million like it warn't nothing. But even if you give a million and don't give it free-hearted, it is like nothing. Do you get what I am trying to say?"

"You are dealing in very high figures," I said, "so it sounds complicated. Nevertheless, since you have been standing at this bar for the last half-hour with an empty glass, I will give you a beer."

"I accept," said Simple. "Thank you."

"Don't mention it," I said. "It's nothing."

"Nothing is everything," said Simple, "when it comes from the heart. But even a glass of beer when it don't come from the heart tastes like nothing. You know, I told you before, I were a passed-around child, so I know when

something tastes like nothing. Even a Sunday dinner can
taste like nothing, and if you are a little small child, you
wonder why.

"One Sunday when I was little down in Virginia, even
before they nicknamed me Simple, I went looking in the
rain that dusk-like evening for something I did not know
what, somewhere I did not know where. Seems like I was
looking for somebody, I did not know who, because I had
just come out of a house full of peoples but they was
lonesome to me, and I was lonesome to them. Nobody put
me out of no house that day, and they had give me plenty
to eat, but I just went off in the rain by myself walking
down the street looking. I went down a street with big
rich fine houses setting on lawns under trees where poor
folks did not live nor colored. And I thought nobody lonesome like me ever lived there, which maybe was wrong. I
were only a little small child and I did not know then that
rich folks sometimes might be lonesome, too, in a house
full of loneliness even when their big fine house is full of
peoples.

"Sundays my aunt sent me to Sunday School and I
looked at Jesus who were white on a Sunday School card,
and at Moses who were white, and Mary Mother of God
also white, and I were lonesome in that colored Baptist
Church in Virginia with Sunday School cards that were
white—and me not the color of nobody I knew with white
relatives. Jesus was the color of the white folks that black
folks worked for in our town. Jesus had long straight hair
that hung down to the neck of His robes, and I wondered
what kind of drawers Jesus wore under His robes. All the
men on them Sunday School cards had on robes, and I
wondered if they wore underneath pants or what. I also
wondered why Bible peoples wore their hair so long. Also,

how did an angel with such long wings, ever set down?
On the Sunday School cards the angels were always
standing up, else flying. These such thoughts I thought
setting in Sunday School, until the old lady teacher said,
'Now let's all sing, "Jesus loves me, that I know, because
the Bible tells me so." ' We also sang 'Jesus Wants Me for
a Sunbeam.' Then she said, 'Let us pray.'

"I pictured in my mind a white God listening to me
praying. And I wondered if he cared anything about a
little colored boy's prayers, or did he just listen to the
peoples in the big fine houses with the porches and lawns
and trees and the pretty lamps with big shades in their
windows at night. Did he listen to me setting in Sunday
School wondering what kind of drawers Jesus wore? Anyway, I was walking that day in the rain. And I was thinking about my old aunt who was not really my aunt, but
who was my father's stepfather's sister and who took me
in and took care of me while my mother was away
somewhere. I were a passed-around child. While my
mother was not there and my father was not there and
they was separated, I were left with whoever would take
care of me when they was not there.

"Nobody was mean to me, and I do not know why I had
that left-out feeling, but I did, I guess because nobody
ever said, 'You're mine,' and I did not really belong to
nobody. When I got big and grown up, I took for my
theme song in my early manhood years that old record of
Billie Holiday's which says, 'God bless the child that's got
his own.' If I had a child, be he or she girl or boy, I would
make sure I kept that child with me and it were my own
and I were its own. I would make sure it did not want to
go back home, even when it came dinnertime and you was
hungry.

"Since I married my second wife, Joyce, I do not have that left-lonesome feeling so much any more. But it took me a long time to find somebody you want to come home to where the house does not feel empty even with somebody in it. It is bad for a full-grown man to come home to somebody who is not there, even if they have got dinner ready. For a little small child, it is worse—that nobody-home-that-belongs-to-you feeling. Even if the house is full of peoples, it is not enough for them to just be there.

"If they do not have a little love for whoever lives in the house with them, it is a empty house. If you have somebody else living in the house with you, be it man, woman, or child, relative or friend, adopted or just taken in, even if it is just a roomer paying rent—even if you give them no money nor a piece of bread and not anything—if you got a little love for whoever it is, it will *not* be a empty house. But if nobody cares, it is an empty house. I have lived in so many empty houses full of peoples, I do not want to live in a crowded empty house no more."

THE BLUES

"I do not know why so many young folks these days and times do not like the blues," said Simple. "They like Rock and Roll, and Rock and Roll ain't nothing much but a whole lot of blues with sometimes a Boogie beat mixed in. Rock and Roll is seventy-two-and-one-half percent blues. But it don't have so many different kinds of expressions as does the blues! The blues can be real sad, else real mad, else real glad, and funny, too, all at the same time. I ought to know. Me, I growed up with the blues. Facts is, I heard so many blues when I were a child until my shadow was blue. And when I were a young man, and left Virginia and runned away to Baltimore, behind me came the shadow of the blues. Oh, if I was a singer man, I could sing me some blues! But I never was much on voice. Still and yet I can holler:

> The blues ain't nothing
> But a good woman on your mind.
> I say, blues ain't nothing
> But a good woman on your mind.
> But your potatoes is gone
> When the frost has killed the vine.
> If you see Corinna,
> Tell her to hurry home.

> Simple ain't had no loving
> Since Corinna's been gone.
> Blues, blues, blues, please
> Do not come my way.
> Gimme something else, Lord,
> Besides the blues all day!

"Do you remember that one?" asked Simple.

" 'Caledonia' sounds something like it," I said.

"Sure do," said Simple. "Corinna and Caledonia must have been sisters. So many blues is about womens.

> Did you ever see a
> One-eyed woman cry?
> She can cry so good just
> Out of that one old eye.
> I was raised in Texas,
> Schooled in Tennessee.
> Can't no little bitty woman
> Make a fool out of me.

And from that you go into one that Old Blind Lemon used to sing:

> I got so many womens I
> Cannot call their name.
> Some of them is crossed-eyed
> But they see me just the same.
> Blues, blues, blues,
> Blues, how-do-you-do?
> I would be blue but
> I got a mojo in my shoe.

GOD'S OTHER SIDE

"Some Negroes think that all one has to do to solve the problems in this world is to be white," I said, "but I never understood how they can feel that way. There are white unemployed, just as there are black unemployed. There are white illiterates, just as there are blacks who can hardly read or write. The mere absence of color would hardly make this world a paradise. Whites get sick the same as Negroes. Whites grow old. Whites go crazy."

"Some of us in Harlem do not have sense enough to go crazy," said Simple. "Some Negroes do not worry about a thing. But me, well, Jim Crow bugs me."

"Bigotry disturbs me, too," I said, "but prejudice and segregation alone do not constitute the root of *all* evil. There are many nonracial elements common to humanity as a whole that create problems from the cradle to the grave regardless of race, creed, color, or previous condition of servitude."

"But when you add a black face to all that," said Simple, "you have problem's mammy. White folks may be unemployed in this American country, but they get the first chance at the first jobs that open up. Besides, they get seniority. Maybe some white folks cannot read or write, but if they want to go to Ole Miss to learn to read or write, they can go without the President calling up the United States Army to protect them. Sure, white folks gets sick, but they don't have to creep in the back door of the hospital down South for treatment like we does. And when they get old, white folks have got more well-off sons and daughters to take care of them than colored folks have. Most old white folks when they get sick can suffer in comfort, and when they die they can get buried without going in debt. Colored folks, most in generally, do not have it so easy. I know because I am one."

"You let yourself be unduly disturbed by your skin," I said. "Sometimes I think you are marked by color—just as some children are born with birthmarks."

"My birthmark is all over me," said Simple.

"Then your only salvation is to be born again."

"And washed whiter than snow," declared Simple. "Imagine all my relatives setting up in heaven washed whiter than snow. I wonder would I know my grandpa were I to see him in paradise? Grandpa Semple crowned in Glory with white wings, white robe, white skin, and golden slippers on his feet! Oh, Grandpa, when the chariot swings low to carry me up to the Golden Gate, Grandpa, as I enter will you identify yourself—just in case I do not know you, white and winged in your golden shoes? I might be sort of turned around in heaven, Grandpa."

"What on earth makes you think you are going to heaven?" I asked.

"Because I have already been in Harlem," said Simple.

"How often do you go to church?" I asked.

"As often as my wife drags me," said Simple. "The last two times I was there the minister preached from the text, 'And I shall sit on the right hand of the Son of God.' Me, half asleep, I heard that much from the sermon. And it set me to wondering why it is nobody ever wants to set on the *left*-hand side of God? All my life, from a little small child in Virginia right on up to Harlem, in church I have been hearing of people setting on the right-hand side of God, never on the left. Now, why is that?"

"When a guest comes to dine, you always seat him or her on your right—that is the main guest sits there," I said. "The right-hand side is the place of honor, granted always to the lady, or the oldest, or the most distinguished person present. The right side is the place of honor."

"I would be glad to set on any old side," said Simple, "were I lucky enough to get into the Kingdom. Besides, if everybody is setting on the right-hand side of God that says they are going to set there, that right-hand side of God would be really crowded. One million Negroes and two million white folks must be setting already on the right. How is there going to be room on that side for anybody else?"

"In the Kingdom there is infinite room, whichever side is chosen," I said.

"No matter how much room there is," said Simple, "that right side of the Throne is crowded by now. I see no harm in setting on the left. God must turn His head that way once in a while, too."

"I suppose He does," I said. "But if you have your choice, why not sit on the right?"

"Just because everybody else is setting there," said Simple. "I would like to be different, and set on the left-hand side all by myself. I expect I would get a little more of God's attention that way—because when He turned around toward me, nobody would be there but me. On His right-hand side, like I said, would be setting untold millions. And all of them folks would be asking for something. God's right ear must be so full of prayers, He can hardly hear himself think. Now me, on the left-hand side, I would not ask for nothing much, were I to get to heaven. And if I did ask for anything, I would whisper soft-like, 'Lord, here is me.'

"Were the Lord to grant me an answer, and say, 'Negro, what do you want?' I would say, 'Nothing much, Lord. And if you be's too busy on your right-hand side to attend to me now, I can wait. I tried to leave my business on earth pretty well attended to—but just in case my wife, Joyce, needs anything, look after her, Lord. I love that girl. Also my Cousin Minnie—protect her from too much harm in them Lenox Avenue bars which she do love beyond the call of duty. Also my junior nephew, F. D., that I helped to raise when he first come to Harlem in his teens, who is out of the Army and married now, show F. D. how to get along with his wife and be a good young man, and not pattern himself too much after me, who were frail as to being an example for anybody.

" 'The peoples that I love, Lord, is the only ones I whispers into Your left ear about. If I was on Your right side, which is crowded with all the saints who ever got to Glory, me who ain't much, might have to holler from afar off for You to hear me at all. Me, who never was nobody, am glad just to be setting on Your left side, Lord—me, Jesse B. Semple, on the left-hand side of the Son of God! And I wants to whisper just *one* thing to You, God—I hope You loves the ones I love, too.' "

COLOR PROBLEMS

"Two things I would hate to be in Harlem right now is a light-skin Negro and a black cop," said Simple. "If it is true what the downtown papers said about some Black Blood Brotherhood out to kill all white folks, how can a near-white Negro the complexion of Adam Powell be sure that the Brotherhood might not make a mistake and kill him too?"

"What a thought!" I cried.

"Yes," said Simple. "And as to the colored polices in these days and times with civil rights at the boiling point, if a Negro cop tries to arrest somebody doing wrong to get his rights, that cop is liable to be taken as a traitor to his race, to integration, freedom and also equality. Yes, sir! In fact, any colored cop who has to arrest a civil rights demonstrator these days must feel bad, because I know that cop wants his rights the same as any other Negro. I would feel bad, too, would'n you?"

"Indeed, the position of the colored policemen in the civil rights battle must be difficult," I said. "I saw a photograph in the papers of a colored policeman in a Southern town arresting some colored teen-agers who were picketing a white movie theatre to which that colored policeman himself could not buy a ticket. I wonder what would you do if you were a Negro policeman in such a case!"

"I would refuse to make an arrest," said Simple. "I would not be a traitor to my race just in order to be a cop. In most Southern towns which have Negroes on the police forces, colored polices do not dare to arrest a white person. Colored cops is limited to making colored arrests."

"The police force, whatever the nationality of its individuals, should be color-blind," I said.

"What is and what *should be* is two different things," said Simple. "Harlem is so full of white cops with white faces and white viewpoints that when some of them see me, they see red because I am *not* white. So when a black cop sees me, he should not look through white eyes. I am his brother—even when I am walking on a picket line and do not move fast enough to satisfy the police commissioner. Colored cops should know why I do not move any faster—because I have been so slow in getting my rights to belong to that white union I am picketing which bars me from earning a living even on a project built by the city with my tax money. A colored cop ought not to be so quick to arrest me when that cop's own son cannot get into the union, either. That cop knows his tax money and mine is being spent to build government buildings where colored plumbers cannot even install a toilet."

"I admit the dilemma of Negro police in the face of the civil rights struggle is tough. In fact, they face a *double* dilemma."

"I would not like to be a colored cop in the face of no such double," said Simple. "It would break my heart to have to arrest my own teen-age son or his friends, or to arrest these young white students who is fighting and picketing and marching with us for civil rights. Fact is, I would not arrest any of them."

"Are you advocating disobedience to law on the part of Negro policemen?"

"When the law is not on the side of civil rights, then the law is not right, it's white," said Simple. "And if I was a light-complexioned Negro—instead of being dark as I am—I would be afraid some of these kids in Harlem that the papers is calling American Mau Maus might take *me* as being white. And these mixed couples living in Harlem, colored mens married to white womens, and white mens married to colored womens? Suppose Sammy Davis lived in Harlem or Lena Horne—and both of them are married white? I met a light-skin Negro friend of mine, a man, the other night who looks white. Some dark Negro he did not even know said to him in a bar, 'What are you doing up here in Harlem?'

"The light-skin man said, 'I was born in Harlem, and I live in Harlem, and I am as black as you.'

"The dark fellow said, 'You better show it then, and get a sun tan.'

"My friend said that for the first time in his life, he was scared of his own people. He said Adam Powell better come back home from Washington and make a speech about how black Negroes should not bother light Negroes in Harlem, since we is *all* blood brothers. Do you reckon them stories in the papers was true about the Blood Brothers being out to do white folks in?"

"Newspaper headlines make things seem many times worse than they are in reality," I said. "But whites in Harlem are apprehensive, that's sure. It's regrettable."

"Maybe that old saying, 'A dark man shall see dark days,' ought to be changed to include dark cops, *light* Negroes, and white mens. Me, I am glad I am neither," said Simple.

THE MOON

"Love is a many-splintered thing," sang Simple, standing at the bar. "If my heart had rings in it like a tree log, you could tell how many loves I have had—I mean of the heart not the body. I used to fall in love with movie stars when I were a young boy, and you know I could not get near no movie star, they being white and way up yonder on the screen and me in a Jim Crow balcony down in Virginia. When I come to Baltimore as a young man, setting in a Jim Crow theatre on Pennsylvania Avenue, the first colored movie star I fell in love with was Nina Mae McKinney, who was showing herself off in a picture called *Hallelujah*, which were fine. Nina Mae were so beautiful she made my heart ache. Then I fell in love with Isabel, who became my first wife, and I forgot about movie stars. Isabel kept my nose to the grindstone, so I did not have neither time or money to go to movies.

"With Isabel it was always *buy* this, *buy* that, *buy* a icebox, *buy* a toaster, *buy* a washing machine which runs by electricity so I don't have to wash by hand, *buy* me a fur coat, *buy* me a boxer-dog. Isabel sure could want more things than you could shake a stick at. And when I was bought out, I was put out. Thank God, my present wife, Joyce, is not a *buy-me* girl, neither a *gimme* woman.

Joyce works, too. We puts our money together, what she makes and what I make, and run on a budget. It's me who has to say 'gimme' to my wife now to even get beer money from that budget. We are saving to buy a house. But Joyce wants to go to the suburbans. I wants to stay in Harlem. So there's a conflict."

"And who will win?" I inquired.

"My wife," said Simple, "but not without a struggle. I can see myself now shoveling snow and cutting lawns so far from Harlem I can't even smell a pig's foot. Me, I do not want to go to *no* suburbans, not even Brooklyn. But Joyce wants to integrate. She says America has got two cultures, which should not be divided as they now is, so let's leave Harlem."

"Don't you agree that Joyce is right?"

"*White is right*," said Simple, "so I have always heard. But I never did believe it. White folks do so much wrong! Not only do they mistreat me, but they mistreats themselves. Right now, all they got their minds on is shooting off rockets and sending up atom bombs and poisoning the air and fighting wars and Jim Crowing the universe."

"Why do you say 'Jim Crowing the universe'?"

"Because I have not heard tell of no Negro astronaughts nowhere in space yet. This is serious, because if one of them white Southerners gets to the moon first, COLORED NOT ADMITTED signs will go up all over heaven as sure as God made little green apples, and Dixiecrats will be asking the man in the moon, 'Do you want your daughter to marry a Nigra?' Meanwhile, the NAACP will have to go to the Supreme Court, as usual, to get an edict for Negroes to even set foot on the moon. By that time, Roy Wilkins will be too old to make the trip, and me too."

"But perhaps the Freedom Riders will go into orbit on

their own," I said. "Or Harlem might vote Adam Powell into the Moon Congress."

"One thing I know," said Simple, "is that Martin Luther King will *pray* himself up there. The moon must be a halfway stop on the way to Glory and King will probably be arrested. I wonder if them Southerners will take police dogs to the moon?"

"You are a great one for fantasy," I said, "maybe stemming from your movie-going days."

"Which is when I first discovered that love is a many-splintered thing," sighed Simple.

DOMESTICATED

"My Cousin Minnie, beings as she is temporarily alone again, tells me she is looking for a boy friend these days who means business," said Simple. "And what Minnie means by *business* is when she asks a man, 'Baby, can you pay my rent? That kitchenette of mine costs me $155 a month, which is without gas—so he who lives there must share.' That's what Minnie says."

"Economics plays a large part in love in Harlem these days," I agreed. "He who would woo, must shell out, too."

"Which is one reason I do not stray at all since I been married," said Simple. "I cannot afford it. My budget do not allow for me living with nobody but my wife, or drinking with nobody but myself, and playing more than one number a day, combinated. I am a man. Minnie is a lady. I takes care of myself. Minnie needs taking care of. I do not blame my boon cousin for asking what a man's finances are before she chooses a permanent friend. To get a good woman, any man must pay, and my Cousin Minnie is not to be sneezed at. Brains run in the Semple family."

"Your Cousin Minnie ought to make some man a good wife," I said.

"In the far distant future, when she gets tired of setting on bar stools," Simple replied. "Right now, let Minnie play the field. She's still young. If she picks a winning horse, she can always get hitched before the season ends. If the man is a sometimer, she can let him go and wipe the slate clean to chalk up new bets."

"It is too bad love and money have to be so mixed up," I said, "especially for a woman."

"Landlords are not interested in love—just money. They wants their rent each and every month," said Simple. "When a man and a woman are both working, they can share the rent. But Minnie is the type that likes to set down on a man. That is her way of 'making him a home,' as she puts it. She claims that if she goes out and works, too, the home is nothing but an empty shell. Minnie has got the same ideas as a rich white lady."

"I don't blame her," I said, "if she can get away with it. But most colored men hardly make enough to take care of themselves, let alone a family—which is one of the regrettable facts of Negro economics. Yet Minnie has the right idea. A woman should be a wife, not a work horse."

"She should have a man's dinner ready when he comes home," said Simple. "It is hard for a man to love a woman on an empty stomach."

"You are the old-fashioned type," I said. "You want your wife to work outside the home, and inside it too."

"I wants my dinner at night."

"Then you ought to hire a cook."

"I married one," said Simple. "Joyce has to eat the same as me. Since women have to cook for themselves, they might as well cook for their man too."

"Also, you expect your wife to keep the house clean?"

"Joyce swears she cannot live in filth, for which I am grateful," said Simple, "as I never was one for house cleaning, myself. I might sweep a little on Sunday. And lately

Joyce has bulldozed me into scrubbing the linoleum. I also last week washed the front windows."

"Gradually getting domesticated," I said. "I am glad Joyce can get something out of you on Sundays, as late as you stay up sporting around on Saturday."

"Late?" said Simple. "I go home at closing time. I must love Joyce, as much as I have changed since I got married. Comes midnight no matter where I am, I think about my wife."

"You are probably scared she is thinking about you," I said.

"How did you guess it?" asked Simple. "I am going home right now before Joyce gets ready to raise sand. If you see my Cousin Minnie, tell her Jess Semple has been here and gone. Good night!"

BOMB SHELTERS

"It is wise to keep one eye open," said Simple, "even when you are asleep."

"To what are you referring now?" I asked, leaning on the bar as Simple gazed (with a hint my way) at his empty glass.

"The trickeration going on in this world," said Simple.

"What trickeration?" I inquired.

"Atom bomb shelters," said Simple. "Our landlord last week came talking to me about he was going to have to raise our rent in order to build us a bomb shelter in the back yard. Now you know, Harlem landlords have no intentions of building no bomb shelters for their roomers. With 50-11 people living in each and every rooming house, even if the law required it, how could landlords build enough shelters for every roomer? And if roomers built their own shelters—me and Joyce living in a kitchenette, for instance—suppose we build a bomb shelter in the landlord's back yard. How would we keep the other roomers out in case of a raid? Them people on the ground floor would beat us to our shelter before we could get downstairs. They has an ageable grandmother in their family downstairs.

"Now, what kind of a gentleman would I be if I said,

'Grandma, you cannot go in my shelter'? How would I sound saying to an old lady, 'If you come in, *I* have to stay out. This mail-order shelter I got is only assembled for my wife and me?' How would that sound? But them mail-order shelters is only big enough for two.

"Of course, I could always put it up to Joyce, who tells me I must be a gentleman, come what may. With the atom sirens sounding, standing at the door of my shelter, I would say, 'Joyce, you are my wife. Does you wish me or Grandma to accompany you inside this shelter? Should I give way to a nice old lady and stand outside and meet my death, or go underground with you and leave somebody else's grandma out? You have told me in the past, "Ladies first. Be a gentleman." What do you say now, Joyce?'

"Of course, Joyce might be real noble and say, 'Age before beauty.'

"Then I would say, 'Joyce, I know you do not mean I should go in.'

"Whereupon Joyce would say, 'This is no time for joking, Jess Semple.'

"So I would say, 'I will be a gentleman then, Joyce, and let Grandma go down in the shelter with you—although she is no relation to us.'

"I can just see Joyce turning as pale as her complexion will permit, at the thought of losing me, burnt to an atom, outside the door.

"But by then Grandma would take my arm and say, 'Son, you know I cannot go in that shelter without my grandchildren, Martha Mae, Ellen, and Johnny-Baby here.'

"Sure enough, if I looked back there would stand all them little ones in Grandma's family, scared as they could be, out there in the middle of the night at the door of *my* atom bomb shelter, clutching onto Grandma. Behind them would stand also their mother and father.

"Then one of the young ones would start crying, 'I don't want to go in that cave without my mama.'

"I would say, 'This shelter was built for two, honey. Your grandma, three children, and your mama makes five—not counting my wife, Joyce. Who can figure that out?'

"Whereupon, the big old Negro what fathered all them children—but neglected to build them a shelter—would say, 'Don't *nobody* count Papa?'

"I would yell, 'No, I do not count Papa. Before I would let you in my shelter, I would fight you. You have seen me in the corner bar ninety-nine times and have not treated me to a beer yet.'

" 'Do you want to make something out of it?' he would say, balling up his fists.

" 'I'll fight you barehanded,' I would say.

"But Joyce would scream, 'Jess Semple! With death staring you in the face, do you want to make a commotion?'

" 'I do,' I would say, taking off my coat. 'I'll fight him here and now.'

"But just at that moment, believe it or not, the all-clear signal would sound, the sirens would stop, and the radios would start blaring, 'Danger is past.' The warning must have been a false alarm. Grandma and that family downstairs would all go trooping back into the house.

"Joyce would throw her arms around my neck and say, 'Thank God, you're saved, Jess Semple! But let's tear that shelter down tomorrow. I could not go in there and leave them children and Grandma outside. Neither could I leave you outside, baby, Jess darling, my life!'

" 'Nor could I leave you,' I would say, hugging her in my arms as close as white on rice.

" 'So let's just tear our shelter down,' Joyce would say. 'If the bomb does come, let's just *all die* neighborly.' Then Joyce and me would go back in the house—our problem solved. Anyhow, we could not go in a shelter and leave Grandma outside."

GOSPEL SINGERS

"It looks," said Simple, "like the churches are buying up half the old movie theatres in Harlem and turning them into temples. Lenox Avenue, Seventh Avenue, Amsterdam, all up and down, it is getting so you can't tell a theatre from a church any more. Now the ministers have got their name up in lights out front just like movie actors. Have you noticed?"

"I have," I said. "I guess television is driving the neighborhood movie houses out of business."

"Yes, and churches are taking over," said Simple. "The church will be here when the movies are gone, that's a sure thing. But old-time store-front churches are going out of style. From now on, it looks like you will have to call them *movie-front* churches—except that the box office has turned into a collection plate, and the choir is swinging gospel songs. Money is being made, just one collection after another."

"You are not opposed to churches taking up collections, like other institutions, are you? They have to pay rent, light, heat, plus ministers' fees."

"I am not opposed," said Simple, "not when they put on a good show."

" 'Show' is hardly the word to use in reference to religion," I said. "Do you think so?"

"That is the way some of churches advertise their
gospel singers these days," said Simple. "I seed a poster
outside a church last night, SISTER MAMIE LIGHTFOOT AND
HER GOSPEL SHOW, and they were charging one dollar to
come in, also programs cost a quarter, and you had to buy
one to pass the door."

"Did you go in?"

"I did, and it were fine! Four large ladies in sky-blue
robes sung 'On My Journey Now,' sung it and swung it,
real gone, with a jazz piano behind them that sounded
like a cross between Dorothy Donegan and Count Basie.
Them four sisters started slow, then worked it up, and
worked it up, and worked it up until they came on like
gang busters, led by Sister Lightfoot. Then they started
walking up and down the aisle from the pulpit to the rear,
making out like they really was on their journey to the
Promised Land—and the church fell in. They did the last
part over about seventeen times. Folks leaped, jumped,
hollered, and shouted, and started marching too. Then
they took up a collection for the benefit of Sister Lightfoot. The plates were overflowing. I put in my dollar myself."

"You mean after you had already paid a dollar at the
door?"

"I were so moved that I did not mind contributing
again," said Simple. "Besides there were a young Negro
there named McKissick who rocked the rafters. That boy
can stone sing a song! To tell the truth, gospel singers
these days put more into a song than lots of night club
stars hanging onto a microphone looking like they are on
their last legs. Besides, you can hear a gospel singer two
blocks off, singing and swinging, even without a mike. In
the past I have heard Mahalia, the Ward Singers, Sallie

Martin, Princess Stewart, Elder Beck, James Cleveland, the Dixie Hummingbirds, the Davis Sisters, also the Martin Singers, and I am telling you, the music that these people put down cannot be beat. It moves the spirit—and it moves the feet. It is gone, man, solid gone! Which is why I has no objections to paying at the door, then shelling out some more when I get inside even if they do invest most of it in automobiles.

"As good as them gospel peoples sing, why should they not ride on rubber—of any kind they want from Cadillacs to Jaguars. Why, I saw a quartet of five come driving up to a church in Harlem once, and each one of them singers in the quartet was driving a different kind of car, and each car were *fine!* Them five boys got out of them five fine cars and went into the church and started singing 'If I Can Just Make It In,' meaning into the Kingdom. They also sung, 'I Cannot Get There by Myself,' and everybody said, 'Help 'em, Jesus! Help 'em!' Which the congregation did by contributing a dollar, or a dollar and a half. Them boys took home a bushel of money.

"Another song I like is 'Move On Up a Little Higher,' also 'Precious Lord, Take My Hand.' Don't you? Some of them large colored sisters can really sing such songs. We have some *great* gospel singers in this land. They are working in the vineyards of the Lord and digging in His gold mines. Why, some gospel singers these days are making so much money that when you hear them crying, 'I Cannot Bear My Burden Alone,' what they really mean is, 'Help me get my cross to my Cadillac.' Which is O.K. by me, as long as they keep on singing like they do. Good singers deserve their just rewards, both in this world and in the other one. Yes, they do!"

"You are really a gospel *aficionado*," I said.

"Whatever that means, I do like gospel. But take my wife, Joyce, she is not too much moved by it, although she appreciates Mahalia. Joyce goes for opera—which sounds like a lot of squalls and squawks to me."

"What operas?" I asked.

"Any opera," said Simple. "But what I am meaning now is them that Joyce listens to on the radio. My wife is the most opera-listening woman I know. Me, I do not care much for it."

"Probably because you do not understand opera," I said.

"They are all in Italian," said Simple, "and Joyce do not understand Italian neither, yet she loves opera."

"Your wife appreciates the music," I said, "and she probably takes the time and trouble to read the story of *Carmen* or *Tosca* or *Aïda* or what not. Culture may not always be appreciated without preparation. Perhaps if you were to read the libretto of an opera and know its story, you would understand it better."

"But why is all operas in Italian?"

"They are not all in Italian. Wagner's operas are in German, Bizet's in French, Moussorgsky's in Russian, and Menotti's in English," I said.

"Even when operas are in English, they *sound* like they are in Italian," said Simple. "Once I went with Joyce to Carnegie Hall to hear a colored opera presented by Madam Dawson and writ by a famous colored composer, and it sounded to me like it were sung in Yiddish. All the singers were colored. The programs said the opera were in English, so I know it was not Italian. But if you have ever pushed a cart like me down in the garment center with Jewish peoples, you have heard Yiddish. You know it is a language you cannot understand. Since I could not understand this opera, I asked Joyce did she reckon all them colored singers had Jewish singing teachers?

"Joyce said, 'Sh-sss-ss-s! Why do you ask such an absurd question?'

"I said, 'Because I do not understand a word.'

"Joyce said, 'But what tone! What projection! Do you not hear that bel canto?'

"I said, 'Hell, no! I can't oh!' Which made Joyce mad, oh! She began to tell me that she did not see why I had to show my ignorance right there in Carnegie Hall. She said I should not be talking during an aria, anyhow, and that Madam Dawson had put on a fine production.

"I said, 'Everybody sure looks fine down on that stage, most particularly that chick in the low-cut gown with the broach over her navel. She looks sharp.'

" 'She is singing flat,' said Joyce, 'and is the least good in the company.'

" 'I had rather look at her than at that big fat lady singing "Great Google Moogle!" ' I said.

" 'She is not singing "Great Google Moogle," ' cried Joyce. 'She is chanting "Great God of Mercy," crying to a voodoo god to save her lover from death.'

" 'I am glad you told me what it is all about,' I said. But by that time Joyce had turned her back as far as she could on me in them seats we had paid $5.50 per each for to hear that opera. Joyce were listening fluently—maybe she do enjoy that kind of music. But me I don't understand it! I prefers gospel."

"Just because you don't understand a thing, do not make fun of it too harshly, or be too critical of others for liking it. Tastes differ. You go for beer, some go for Bach, some for Goldoni, and some for gospel. As for opera, thousands of people like it. You happen not to be in that number. Yet, if I remember correctly, when Marian Anderson first sang with the Metropolitan Opera you were one of those cheering the loudest, right here at this bar."

"Right!" said Simple. "Right *here* at this bar, not at the opera. Bravo, Marian! Sing, woman, sing! Bartender, set me up a beer. And now that Marian Anderson has retired and put opera and concerts down, I hope she takes up gospel. She could make a million dollars as a gospel singer."

"Don't be ridiculous," I said.

"When was money ever ridiculous?" asked Simple.

NOTHING BUT A DOG

"I once had a no-good husband—went off and left me. Didn't leave me nothing but a dog," Cousin Minnie said to Simple as they sat stool by stool at the bar. "Dog's name were Cargo. He were a black dog, had one white eye. My husband were in the Merchant Marines on a coal vessel sailing out of Norfolk at that time. He brought that little old black mutt back from Trinidad or somewhere. Since that little old hound looked like a load of coal hisself, so black, he named him Cargo.

"Cargo were something! Too affectionate for his own good, that dog. He loved me, but he like to drove me crazy, running off and stuff. He traipsed all over town like his master, and never got runned over. That dog knew a red light from a green one as well as I did. Cargo loved people, but hated dogs. This I never did understand. If I was a dog, I think I would like other dogs. But Cargo's hair bristled. He looked like a walking clothesbrush when he saw one. And he were evil.

"One time Cargo bit a white lady's dog down the street, and got bit in return. They fit, fought, and fit, barked, growled, howled, and bit. Both dogs were right smart chewed up.

"That old white lady come running down to my place and says, 'Your dog bit mine.'

"I said, 'It also seems like your dog bit mine.'

"She said, 'Your dog has no business biting my dog.'

"I said, 'Your dog has got no business biting Cargo.'

"She looked at me. I looked at her. She said, 'Don't be impudent with me.'

"I said, 'Don't you be impudent, neither, madam. I don't know you, and I never seen your dog. What proof you got that my dog bit your dog? Cargo *is* bit—look at his ear. But who bit him, and who exactly he bit, I do not know.'

" 'Do you dispute my word?' asked Old White Lady. 'I say your black dog bit mine.'

" 'Don't you call my dog black,' said I.

" 'Well it is black,' said the lady.

" 'So am I,' I said, 'but don't call me out of my name.'

" 'What is your name?' says Old White Lady, 'because I see where I am going to have to take you to court.'

"I started to tell her, 'Take your mama to court!' But she wouldn't understand, so I just said, 'Did *I* bite your dog?'

" 'Your dog has no license,' says she. 'I will have the Pound come and remove your dog from this street. He's a menace. What was your dog doing in my yard attacking my dog?'

" 'What are you doing at my door yelling at me? I am not a dog. Speak civil, else don't speak to me at all. Cargo, stop rubbing against that lady's leg. She's liable to bite you. Cargo, set down. Madam, I am sorry if my dog bit your dog!'

" 'I am no madam,' yells the lady, indignant-like.

" 'What is you?' I asked.

" 'My name is Mrs. Bertha—'

" 'Mine is Minnie,' I cut her off. 'So, Bertha, time's up.

You go home to your dog and leave me with mine. Goodby!' I shut the door.

" 'I want redress,' said Bertha.

" 'Redress, huh! Colored folks dress—and white folks redress. Cargo, set down! You ain't nothing but a dog.' "

ROOTS AND TREES

"My wife is an intellect," said Simple, "and that club she belongs to is always pursuiting culture. Nothing wrong, except that it takes so much time. Joyce was setting up in the library all last Saturday reading up on that old problem of how to solve the question of 'you can take a Negro out of the country but you can't take the country out of the Negro'—which I say is a lie. Harlem has certainly taken the country out of me. When I first come to the Big Apple, I did not know beans from bull foot. But look at me today—hip, slick, cool, and no fool."

"You manage to hold your own in New York," I said.

"A foothold is all I need," said Simple, "and my hands will hang on. I been hanging on in New York for a right smart while, and intend to stay. I will not return to the country, North or South. No backwoods for me. I am a big-city man myself. My roots is here."

"In other words, urbanized."

"That's a word I heard Joyce use," said Simple. "What her club is studying is how to make the un-urbanized Negro do right and stop throwing garbage out the window, sweeping trash in the street, fussing on the stoop, and cussing on the corner. Joyce says her club is making that a project. To which I said, 'Joyce, I think you-all have bit off more than a ladies' club can chew.'

"To which Joyce answers, 'Well, you men are doing little or nothing about it. What club do you belong to, Jesse B. Semple, that is trying to remedy the disgraceful conditions of adult delinquency here in Harlem? I am not talking about children, but grown delinquent men.'

"I said, 'Baby, do not look at me in that tone of voice. You know I carries myself right, drunk or sober.'

"To which Joyce says, 'To act right yourself is not enough. You must also help others to act right. We are all our brother's keeper—and cousin's, too.'

"I knowed Joyce was referring to my Cousin Minnie, who sometimes do not act like a lady. But I ignored Joyce's last remark. I said, 'Darling, you know I belong to the NAACP, and I would join the Elks if my budget would let me.'

" 'Our club,' says Joyce, 'is an auxiliary of the Urban League, and our president, Mrs. Sadie Maxwell-Reeves, is an officer in the Harlem branch of the League, which has done much to help transpose the rural Negro to big-city ways, the Southern customs to Northern manners.'

" 'Then that is where I should send my Cousin Minnie,' says I, 'to your club—to see if you-all can't take some of that down-home loudness out of her mouth. Minnie would be a right nice woman if she were not so loud.'

" 'Minnie also needs a job adjustment,' said Joyce.

" 'A job—period!' says I, 'but the kind of job where she does not have to go on time.'

" 'There are no such jobs in an urban community,' says Joyce. 'In the city, folks work by clocks, not by how they feel when they get up in the morning.'

" 'That I learned early,' I agreed. 'Before I married you and sobered up, Joyce, I learned to go to work on time, hangover or no hangover, else be fired. Northern white folks is harder on a late Negro than they are down South.'

" 'That is because the whole South runs late,' said Joyce. 'But up here in the free North—'

" 'A man ain't free to be late,' I said, cutting her off.

"But once Joyce latches onto a subject, there is no cutting her off. Joyce said, 'Jesse B., I want you to help me form a Block Club.'

" 'A what?' says I.

" 'A club to keep this block clean.'

" 'Baby,' I said, 'it would take more than a club. It would take artillery, tanks, and the state militia.'

" ' I am not joking,' said Joyce. 'Just theory and no action gets society nowhere, so Sadie Maxwell-Reeves said in her talk at the All-State Women's Convention last month, where she were the only colored woman to appear at the windup session. The message she brought back to us here in Harlem was, *action and more action*. Jess Semple, we women are marching into action. And you men are going to help us.'

" 'Joyce, baby,' I knowed I had better ask, 'what do you want me to do?'

" 'Help us take away their country ways and prepare them for big-city days.'

" 'In plain words,' I said, 'to live in the city, get with the nitty-gritty, wise up and be witty.'

"Joyce did not even smile. All she said was, 'Jess, don't be silly.' So I pulled a long face, too. Now you know I got to try to do what Joyce wants me to do. Next thing you know, Joyce will be president of our Block Club, and *I* am going to help her."

"Amen!" I said.

"Joyce says Harlem has got to let down our roots where

we are," said Simple, "and let our trees grow tall. I wonder where is the tallest tree in the world, anyhow?"

"I have seen some pretty tall trees among the redwoods in California," I said, "and some very tall palms in Africa."

"But there has to be some tree on earth somewhere that is taller than any other tree anywhere," said Simple, "maybe just a tiny smidgen taller, say a quarter of an inch, or maybe only an eighth of an inch, but that little tiny bit extra of a fraction of an inch would make it the tallest tree, taller than any other tree in the world. And it could be proud. I wonder where that tree is? Probably in Africa —and, if so, the black race can be proud of having the tallest tree in the world."

"Nonsense," I said. "How can any race be proud of something it did not create? You know that song that so many singers moo and croon and bawl over about 'only God can make a tree'? How can a man be proud of a tree that just grew?"

"Well, at least he did not cut it down," said Simple. "Say, what do you think it would be like to be married to the tallest woman in the world? A little short woman is hard enough to keep in harness. And even a medium-size woman like my wife, Joyce, I am sometimes afraid to tackle. But the tallest woman in the world, unless she was married to one of the Globe Trotters, would be something for a man to handle. It is funny how God lets some folks grow so tall like Wilt Chamberlain, and others grow so short like Sammy Davis, and me so in-between with neither shortness or tallness. Nobody makes admiration over me no kind of way—except my wife. Sharp-tempered as she can be sometimes, there is other times when Joyce says to me, 'Baby, you are the sweetest man on earth!' And she looks at me with them sweet, wonderful admiring

eyes of hers; then I feel like the tallest tree in the world—
that tree that is maybe just one little one-eighth of an inch
taller than any other tree anywhere in the world. Me, I
am that tree. Oh, friend, the power of a sweet kind word
to keep you tall."

FOR PRESIDENT

"What is this the big shots are saying about us Negroes being cool because there might be a Negro President in the year 2011 in the U.S.A., huh? If I am going to run for President, I want to run now—because by 2011 I would be *too* cool.

"One time at the Apollo Theatre in Harlem I heard Jackie Moms Mabley talking about the good old days. She said, 'What good old days? I was there. There wasn't no good old days.' I agrees with her. First thing I remember in my youthhood was Depression. Everybody was on Relief that could get on Relief. But if you was colored down South, you had a hard time getting on Relief, even getting in a CCC Camp were you a teen-age boy. Them things was for white. If you be black—be hungry. Be black don't look for help from the Government. Be black just stay black and die. What good old days? When?

"Then come the war. Suppose you wanted to wear one of them pretty Navy uniforms, or fly in the sky. You better be white—else cook or scrub in the Navy, and not fly in no sky. No Negroes in the Air Force. Not then. Suppose you want to give your blood to the Red Cross. Un-uh! No black blood accepted. When they finally did, they put it in black cans. And just try to work in a war plant down South. What good old days?

"Also in war days, try to get on a train down South to go somewhere else. The one COLORED coach was always crowded when it come through your town. 'No more room for Nigras,' the conductor would cry. The good old days? When? They didn't want you in the South and they didn't want to let you out.

"You finally got up North. You sleep six in a room. Work on the docks loading ammunition, with the union not sure it wants you or don't. Ride that long subway to Harlem. Everything so high uptown it uses up all your money in no time. What good old days? Can't even be a clerk in your own butcher shop where you trade in Harlem, or a bartender in the bar where you spend your money. Good old days? When? Where?

"Now they come talking about a cooling-off period. Were I any cooler, I would be dead. How long must I wait? Like the blues says, 'Can I get it now, or must I hesitate?' I am still looking for the good old days and they don't come yet.

"Now they tell me I got to wait forty or fifty years to be President. I do not want to wait that long. I want to be President now, because I wishes to decree Alabama, Georgia, Mississippi, and Louisiana out of the Union. I wishes to give them states to the Devil, because it would take fire and brimstone to straighten them out. I would save only the dogs down there because dogs is nothing but dumb animals and I do not believe in sending dogs to hell.

"The Negroes in them states ought to know Judgment Day is coming—so let them make their peace, get away, or else. If they else, let it be like them Freedom Riders. Else in a big way!

"As to cooling off? Me? Cool off from what? I never held

nothing hot. Who has got the guns and dogs and billy clubs and ballots in the South? Who does the lynchings and beatings and mobbings and name-calling? Whose blood rushes to they heads when they see a black face? Who gets hot under the collar when the Supreme Court edicts an edict that don't stick? Who calls every black man *red* that wants a piece of white bread? Suppose I was to run for President? Who would need to cool off most? Not me! Not mine! Not Mose, not Corinna, not Rev. Martin Luther King, neither Rev. Shuttleworth. Them black mens is cool, already coo-oo-ol, cooooooool, Jack, cool! You be cool too, Mr. President. Don't go putting no ideas in my head about running for President. I just might do it *now*. I am Simple."

ATOMIC DREAM

"Man, I had the awfullest dream last night," said Simple.

"What did you dream?" I asked.

"I drempt that in the next war a white woman was running toward an atom bomb shelter, and some Negroes right behind her ran over her and tromped her. The rest of the white folks started to fight the Negroes, but the Negroes ran over them and tromped them, too. When the bomb fell, the shelter was full of Negroes. Why do you reckon I drempt that?"

"You were just acting out your aggressions, as the psychiatrists say, in dreams."

"Doing which?" asked Simple.

"Getting rid of your hostilities," I said, "working out your own evil by way of a dream. Where did this fantasy of yours take place, North or South?"

"You know it was up North," said Simple. "There wouldn't be no Negroes running over no white woman—by accident or otherwise—down South. In fact, the South would probably have no bomb shelters for Negroes in the next war, anyhow. If they did, it would be a little old Jim Crow shelter in Uncle Tommy's back yard meant just for handkerchief heads. The Freedom Riders would have to ride awhile to get in out of the fallout."

"Do you mean to tell me the white South would be so inhumane as to build public bomb shelters with signs up WHITE ONLY, and none for Negroes? What kind of people live in Dixie?"

"You go down there and see," said Simple. "You Northern Negroes do not know what Jackson or Birmingham is like. It is a bo-biddling! But lemme finish telling you about my dream. When I got down in that bomb shelter, who should be down there but Lena Horne singing the 'Wee Small Hours' blues. Lena was standing on top of an air cooler belting it out like she does at the Waldorf. 'In the wee small hours when the one you love is gone.' And the rest of the Negroes was standing around whooping and hollering just as if they was on Lenox Avenue in the Old Colony Bar and Grill. About that time a minister stood up and said, 'Ain't you-all got no respect for death? You should be kneeling and praying instead of singing and shouting the blues!' But nobody heard him, so he sat down again and started patting his foot himself."

"Where was your wife?" I asked.

"She was completely left out of that dream," said Simple.

"Further proof that you are in need of psychiatry, leaving your wife out in a time like that."

"It were only a dream," said Simple. "In real life, I would have kept Joyce with me, bomb or no bomb. But that night in my dream Joyce were not there. She was dreaming her own dreams on the other side of the bed. Me and Lena, we was singing the blues and waiting for the bomb to fall. By and by it fell—BAM! It blowed me down. And I woke up screaming! My dream had turned into a nightmare.

"Joyce just rolled over kind of sleepy-like and said, 'Jess, what is the matter with you, high again? What time did you come home?'

"I said, 'Baby, don't bother me with them kind of questions. I have just been caught in the fallout.'

" 'What fallout?' says Joyce.

" 'Out of bed,' I said."

LOST WIFE

"That man down at the other end of the bar is named Efney," said Simple, "which is a funny name for a man. And he has got a bad deal. Efney's got five children. But no sooner did the oldest one of them get in high school, than his wife had to up and die on him. So Efney brings his old girl friend home to help take care of his children, some of them being only four-five-six years old. But Efney's girl friend is a bar stool girl. Besides she has two children of her own she brought along to Efney's house—which makes seven mouths for him to feed besides him and her. Efney now has his hands full."

"I'll say he has," I affirmed. "Seven children is enough for any man."

"Especially when his wages is less than he would get if all nine of them was to go on welfare. It is better for a man with a big family to be out of work these days than it is for him to work. On relief him and his children get more and bigger checks. Efney's girl friend is still on welfare. Even though she is living with Efney, she keeps her old address and some clothes there, so she can continue to get the checks. The welfare is a wonderful thing for people with more children than they want to take care of. They sure is lucky, since them that gets on welfare need not never get a job."

"Lucky in idleness? I don't agree. Something is wrong with a system where it is more profitable for people *not* to work than it is to work."

"Wrong to *you*," said Simple, "but not to them. Only trouble is Efney's girl friend does not give Efney any money to help feed herself nor her children.

"She says, 'I'm young, so that old Negro is due to take care of me and mine in style. It's me who is doing him a favor, passing my time at his house when I also got my own. He is lucky to latch onto a good-looking pullet like me.' That is what Carlota is going around the bars telling Efney's friends. And his friends is saying, 'That's right,' and wishing they could latch onto Carlota themselves. A friend often ceases to be a friend where womens is involved. I once knew a man's best friend who took his wife away."

"Such cases are not rare," I said. "You are a lucky man. You and Joyce have been married several years now with no sign of a riff, no sign of breaking up."

"The only thing we breaks is our budget," said Simple, "and that not often. But last week I did want some beer to go with the chitterlings Joyce cooks, so she let me have a dollar which she did not mark down on the budget.

"I said, 'Joyce, why do you keep track of all our money so carefully on that budget chart? When it is gone, it is just gone. But if you are going to keep track of everything, why don't you put this beer dollar down?'

"Joyce said, 'I do not want *beer* to show on the budget. That is ex-office.'

"I said, 'Not to me, baby.'

" 'We will never get to buy that house we want in the suburbs,' Joyce says, 'if you keep bursting the budget to buy beer.'

" 'Baby,' I says, 'let's buy a house in Harlem.'

" 'Harlem will soon be nothing but projects and welfare homes,' says Joyce. 'I want to get out where there is leaves and grass and birds. If you loved me, Jess Semple, you would agree with my ambitions.'

"Any time Joyce calls me by my full name, Jess Semple, I know she is serious. So I replies, 'I love you, Joyce, therefore I agrees with your ambitions. But right now, while you set the table, I am going to get my beer.'

" 'Every can of beer is one brick less in the foundations of our future,' says Joyce.

" 'The future of our foundations is you, my wife, my love, my all,' I said. 'Here, take this dollar, put it back in our budget.'

" 'Jesse, go and get your beer,' said Joyce. 'Our future is together. If you need a little beer to cement our bricks, go get it.' Whereupon we kissed. I pity Efney down yonder at the end of the bar who has lost his wife."

SELF-PROTECTION

"She crowned him king of kings," said Simple, "not to mention lord of lords. When my Cousin Minnie hit that man with a beer bottle, he were conked and crowned both all at once. Minnie raised a knot on his head bigger than the Koorinoor Diamond which, I hear, were the biggest diamond ever to be set in a crown."

"Why did your cousin attack the poor fellow in so positive a manner?" I asked.

"That man evidently did not know my Cousin Minnie very well, in spite of the fact he were her steady boy friend since last Thanksgivings," said Simple. "I could see trouble coming before the holidays. In the first place, that man did not buy Cousin Minnie what she wanted for Christmas, which were a fur stole. 'I did not ask him for a fur coat,' said Minnie, 'just a stole—and he did not even get that. Come explaining that his funds was short.'

"Well, I knew Minnie were not happy. Still and yet, it being the season of Peace on Earth, she put up with the joker. She even took him out sporting New Year's Eve on her own money. But, Minnie told me, he got so high before the bells tolled that he wanted to send *her* home. He wanted to stay out and run the streets all the night without being bothered with his old lady. Minnie allowed as how that would never do, not with her money that she had lent him to celebrate in his pocket. Whereupon, one word led to another, so he upped his hand at Minnie. Howsoever, Minnie acted like a lady and backed away. She said, 'Daddy, do not show your color in the Mill Ritz Bar. Let's not end the Old Year on a low note.'

"But Rombow were drunk. He must not have read that sign up over the bar which says WE GROW OLD SO QUICK, BUT GROW WISE SO SLOW. When Rombow upped his hand at Cousin Minnie, he did not use common sense. Minnie is a woman not afraid of man, beast, or devil. She is also no respecter of persons. Minnie were just respecting Rombow because they were out in public, it were New Year's Eve, and the bells had not yet tolled. She also at times tried to be a lady, and she did not wish to end the Old Year on a low note. Minnie said again, 'Rombow, I done spoke nice now, but listen I can raise my voice, too.'

" 'You better not raise it at me,' says Rombow.

"Whereupon, Minnie said, 'What?' so loud everybody in the bar heard her, in spite of all the noise going on plus Ray Charles on the juke box. 'What did you say?' says Minnie.

" 'If you can't hear my voice,' says Rombow, 'you can sure feel my hand.' Whiz! He thought he were fast, but Minnie was faster. When Rombow went to slap her, Minnie squatted. The blow went over her head. When Minnie come up, the nearest beer bottle were in her hand. With this Minnie christened, crowned, and conked Rombow all at once.

"Minnie said, 'If you want to be a king, Rom, I will crown you.' She did. A knot sprung out on Rombow's head the size of a hen's egg. But neither the bottle nor his head broke. However, what little sense he had must have been knocked from his head to his feet, because his feet had sense enough to carry him backwards fast, out of Minnie's way, and when he fell, he fell against the juke box. Rombow were stunned, shook up, shocked, and unconscious.

" 'You must be out of your mind,' said Minnie.

"He were, because when he came to, the bells had tolled. Minnie were surrounded by friends drinking to her health, and everybody had yelled *Happy New Year* so much that they were hoarse.

"It was about that time that I come into the bar, having taken Joyce home from Watch Meeting. I spied my Cousin Minnie and she told me her tale. I said, 'Coz, I should have been here to protect you.'

" 'There is as much difference between *should* and *is*, as between last year and this,' says Minnie. '*Should* has gone down the drain, but *is* is here. I am able to protect myself. Happy New Year to you!' "

HAIRCUTS AND PARIS

"If I had ever been to Paris," said Simple, "I would like to go there one more time once."

"Since you have never been in Paris, how do you know you would?" I asked.

"I know I would, because a friend of mine just came back to New York and told me all about it," said Simple. "He is as dark as me, real colored in complexion, and he said in Paris for the first time in his life, he felt like a *man*."

"I do not see why a Negro has to go all the way to Paris to feel like a man," I said.

"Some do and some don't need to go," said Simple. "Me, I feel like a man anywhere in this American country, because I feel like a man *inside* myself. But some folks are not made like that. Some black men do not feel like men when they are surrounded by white folks who look at them like as if blackness was bad manners or something. It is not bad manners to be black, any more than it is good manners to be white. God made both of us. But white folks in the U.S.A. has got the upper hand—the whip hand—which they have had since the days of slavery. White folks still have a million and one ways of keeping a Negro from feeling like a man—especially if he is a weak

Negro like my friend what went to Paris and stayed a year and for the first time said he felt like a man. Me, in Paris, I would feel like *two* men. That is why I want to go, and return, then go again."

"Once you got to Paris, why would you come back?" I asked.

"To get some corn bread and pigs' feet and greens," said Simple, "which is what my friend said he missed so much in Paris. Also to see Jackie Mabley and Pigmeat Markham and Nipsey Russell at the Apollo, and to hear the Caravans sing gospel songs one more time. Then I would return to Paris and stay another year. My friend says the wonderful thing about Europe is that a Negro can get his hair cut anywhere. That is certainly not true in the U.S.A., where a Negro has to look for a *colored* barbershop—in spite of the Civil Rights Bill—just like in most towns down South he still has to look for a *colored* restaurant in which to eat, a *colored* hospital in which to die, and a *colored* undertaker to get buried by, also a *colored* cemetery to be buried in. They has no such jackassery in Europe."

"What?" I said.

"White folks are not jackasses in Europe," said Simple. "In Europe they accepts colored peoples as human beings. Therefore Negroes can get their hair cut anywhere in any barbershop in Paris, France, or Rome, Italy, or Madrid, Spain. Also Negroes can get shaved. Here in the United States to get shaved, a white barber is liable to cut a colored man's throat instead of trimming his beard. It would take a brave black man to set down in a white barbershop in Memphis, Jackson, Tougaloo, Birmingham, Atlanta, or anywhere else down South. With all the love he has got in his heart, I have never read in no newspaper yet where Rev. Martin Luther King has gone into a white barbershop down South and said, 'I love you, barber. Cut my hair.' Martin Luther King has got more sense than that. He knows prayer might not prevail in no white barbershop in Jackson, Birmingham, Atlanta, or Selma. Or in Boston, either."

"You are right," I said. "My dentist's son, colored, attends college in a small town in Ohio where there is no colored barbershop. This young student has to travel forty miles to Toledo to get his hair cut. The white barbershops near the college will not serve him. They politely claim they do not know how to cut colored hair."

"If white Americans can learn how to fly past Venus, go in orbit and make telestars, it looks like to me white barbers in Ohio could learn how to cut colored hair," said Simple. "But since they also might cut my throat, I prefer to go to Paris, get my hair cut there, then come home for corn bread, and return to Paris again. Even here in Harlem, I thank God for Paris barbers. Amen!"

ADVENTURE

"Adventure is a great thing," said Simple, "which should be in everybody's life. According to the Late Late Show on TV, in the old days when Americans headed West in covered wagons, they was almost sure to run into adventure—at the very least a battle with the Red Skins. Nowadays, if you want to run into adventure, go to Alabama or Mississippi where you can battle with the White Skins."

" 'Go West, young man, go West,' is what they used to say," I said. " 'Pioneers! O pioneers!' cried Whitman."

" 'Go South, young man, go South,' is what I would say today," declared Simple. "If I had a son I wanted to make a man out of, I would send him to Jackson, Mississippi, or Selma, Alabama—and not in a covered wagon, but on a bus. Especially if he was a white boy, I would say, 'Go, son, go, and return to your father's house when you have conquered. The White Skins is on the rampage below the Mason-Dixon line, defying the government, denying free Americans their rights. Go see what you can do about it. Go face the enemy.' "

"You would send your son into the maelstrom of Dixie to get his head beaten by a white cracker or his legs bitten by police dogs?"

"For freedom's sake—and adventure—I might even go

South myself," said Simple, "if I was white. I think it is more important for white folks to have them kind of adventures than it is for colored. Negroes have been fighting one way or another all our lives—but it is somewhat new to whites. Until lately, they did not even know what a COLORED ONLY sign meant. White folks have always thought they could go anywhere in the world they wanted to go. They are just now finding out that they cannot go into a COLORED WAITING ROOM in the Jim Crow South. They cannot even go into a WHITE WAITING ROOM if they are with colored folks. They never knew before that if you want adventure, all you have to do is cross the color line in the South."

"Then, according to you," I said, "the Wild West can't hold a candle to the Savage South any more."

"Not even on TV," said Simple. "The Savage South has got the Wild West beat a mile. In the old days adventures was beyond the Great Divide. Today they is below the Color Line. Such adventures is much better than the Late Late Show with Hollywood Indians. But in the South, nobody gets scalped. They just get cold cocked. Of course, them robes the Klan sports around in is not as pretty as the feathers Indians used to wear, but they is more scary. And though a Klan holler is not as loud as a Indian war whoop, the Klan is just as sneaky. In cars, not on horseback, they come under cover of night. If the young people of the North really want excitement, let them go face the Klan and stand up to it.

"That is why the South will make a man of you, my son,' I would say. 'Go South, baby, go South. Let a fiery cross singe the beard off your beatnik chin. Let Mississippi make a man out of you.' "

"Don't you think white adults as well as white youth should be exposed to this thing?" I asked.

"Of course," said Simple. "If the white young folks go as Freedom Riders, let the white old folks go as sight-seers —because no sooner than they got down there, they would be Freedom Riders anyhow. If I owned one of these white travel bureaus arranging sight-seeing tours next summer to Niagara Falls, Yellowstone Park, the Grand Canyon, and Pike's Peak, I would also start advertising sight-seeing tours to Montgomery with the National Guard as guides, to Jackson with leather leggings as protection against police dogs, to the Mississippi Prison Farms with picnic lunches supplied by Howard Johnson's, and to the Governor's Mansion with a magnolia for all the ladies taking the tour—and a night in jail without extra charge.

"Negroes would be guaranteed as passengers on all tours, so that there would be sure adventures for everybody. My ads would read:

SPECIAL RATES FOR A WEEK-END
IN A TYPICAL MISSISSIPPI JAIL.

Get arrested now, pay later. Bail money not included. Have the time of your lives living the life of your times among the Dixie White Skins. Excitement guaranteed. For full details contact the Savage South Tours, Inc., Jesse B. Semple, your host, wishing you hell."

MINNIE'S HYPE

"When an emergency becomes a habit, that is carrying emergencies too far," said Simple over a glass of brew.

"What emergency are you speaking of now?"

"Borrowing money," said Simple.

"Is your Cousin Minnie annoying you again?"

"*Worrying* me would be a better way of putting it," said Simple. "But if I did not like Minnie, I would not be worried. People you like that are worrisome are the most worrisome kind of all. The one thing wrong with my Cousin Minnie is that she wants to live off of everybody else. Minnie is big, strong, healthy, and bold, so why should she have to make a habit of borrowing from me every time she sees me in this bar? And I am married, too."

"Doesn't Minnie have a job?"

"Not if she can help it," said Simple. "She does not believe in *live and let live*—earning her own living and letting other people earn theirs. She wants them to earn *her* living too. That I refuse to do. She is only an off-cousin of mine, anyhow—not by marriage."

"Blood is thicker than marriage."

"True," said Simple. "But if all who are not married denied their kinship, few people would be related in this

world. To some folks a marriage license is too much
trouble to purchase. And sometimes they can't wait that
long. I do not hold her parents' doings against Minnie,
nohow. She came into this world about the same time I
did down in Virginia. I played with Minnie as a child.
Everybody says she is my cousin, and I take for granted
she is. Still and yet, she do not have to borrow from me
every time she turns around. I am no bank. When Minnie
came up here to Harlem looking for freedom, she must
have thought Freedom was *my* name. I told her in the
beginning I was not named Freedom, my home is not the
North, and my wife did not love in-laws—even if Minnie
is an out-law."

"Go ahead and lend your cousin a couple of bucks," I
said. "It won't hurt you."

"I do not have it," said Simple. "Besides Minnie wants
twenty dollars to pay her rent."

"Oh," I said.

"Oh, is right," said Simple. "Minnie could easy have
paid her rent last week with what she spent getting a
blonde streak put in her hair after it were denatural-
ized."

"Do you begrudge a woman her beauty rites?"

"When it is the man that has to pay for them," said
Simple.

YACHTS

"Sometimes I read in the papers about these peoples with yachtses," said Simple.

"Yachts," I said.

"Yachtses," said Simple.

"*Yachts*," I repeated.

"Anyhow, I would like to own one of them ships," said Simple. "Peoples with their own boats can sail the seas whichever way they want to, and guide their compasses where-so-ever they wishes. It must be wonderful. Nobody can tell you to go thisaway or thataway or whatever way to South America or North. Oh, I wish I was rich and had a yacht. I would sail away from Harlem any time I had a mind to."

"What about your wife?" I said.

"I would sail away if she even looked at me cross-eyed and said, 'Boo!' Womens quarrels too much. If Joyce even said, 'Why don't you hang up your clothes?' I would sail away. No more listening to a whole lot of yap-yap-yap—until I got ready to come back."

"What woman do you think would put up with a gone-away husband most of the time?" I asked.

"I would come sailing back up the Harlem River to Harlem once in a while," said Simple. "When I did, the lights would light up on Lenox Avenue, the radios all would play jump music, and the TVs would show first-run features in my honor. I would be back home. Joyce would kiss me at the door, then run to the stove to cook me the kind of dinner I like, and then—oh, then she would be mine all over again. There is nothing like absence to make the heart grow fonder—so they say, especially a woman's. But I do not believe I will test it."

"No?"

"No! If I had a yacht I would just take Joyce with me. I would not go sailing away all by myself. No."

"The possibility of your getting a yacht and sailing away is so remote, it is hardly likely you will have to face such an eventuality."

"Eventually, Joyce wants a home in the suburbans," said Simple. "She cares nothing for boats. Joyce wants wall-to-wall carpets and a chandelier. That is why Joyce keeps skimming our budget every week to put money in the Carver Bank to buy a house. But houses is so high these days, and mortgages so long to pay off, that I tell her by the time we get the house paid for I will be too old to even mow the lawn. After years of shoveling snow around a house, I would be broke down, anyhow. I prefers to stay here in Harlem in a nice warm apartment where the super shovels the snow, and the janitor sweeps the sidewalks and tends the furnace. All I do is pay the rent. But Joyce declares she wants to own a piece of land all her *own* before she goes to Glory and I go to hell. Joyce wants a little spot of grass, a house with a porch and a porch swing to set and rock in the cool of the evening and hear the crickets chirping in the dark.

"Me, Boyd, I prefers a bar booth; after dark I like a juke box blaring, and lights, lights, lights. I always did like lots of lights, don't know why, lots of people, don't know why, and sometimes a lot of noise. If I had a yacht, I would fill it up with friends. My boat would not only roll but it would rock with music all day long, jump with dancing all night long, smell with pots of food cooking in the galley, biscuits baking in the oven. At all hours there would be lights strung up along the decks, beautiful lights, and on each and every mast flags flying. Every time my boat whistle blowed, it would blow in the key of B-flat, which is the key of the blues.

"Then I would remember the lights shining on Lenox Avenue and how sometimes there might be a flag flying outside the Theresa, maybe on the Fourth of July, or like when Castro was staying there, and I would get homesick for 125th Street. On my fine yacht out yonder on some strange sea where the flying fishes play, I would turn my boat around and head home, yes, I would—*right then and there*—head home to Harlem, U.S.A. Why, I don't know, but I would."

LADYHOOD

"When the man on the next stool last night asked my Cousin Minnie how old she were," said Simple, "she told him, 'Oh, about eleventeen! A man should not ask a lady's age,' she said, 'no more than he should ask if she has a wig on—which I do not tonight. Every strand is my own hair.'

" 'Can you do the Monkey?' asked the man.

" 'Backforwards and forwards,' said Minnie, 'including the Jerk.'

"Whereupon, the man put a quarter in the juke box and him and Minnie performed, until the bartender pointed at the sign NO DANCING and made them stop because it had been five minutes since they had last bought a drink, and the barman's point and purpose is to keep his licker moving."

"I don't see how the bar makes much off of you then," I said to Simple. "But where is your Cousin Minnie tonight?"

"Home resting up until Friday—when the studs get paid," said Simple. "Minnie do not come out on quiet nights. She knows I do not treat relatives—except on Christmas—so she need not look to me to quench her thirst. To be a girl-cousin, Minnie can drink awhile, Jack, yet I have never seen her stagger, let alone reel. Minnie goes out of any bar under her own steam, no matter how many Scotches and sodas she has put away. You have to give it to Minnie—that chick carries her licker well and protects her ladyhood, too. Minnie knows she is a lone woman in this big city—except for me, her Cousin Jess."

"Your Cousin Minnie seems quite self-reliant."

"She is used to making her way in the world, if that is what you mean," said Simple. "If necessary, Minnie will even work to keep her head above water. But not if any other kind of lifeboat or lifeguard is in sight. To be a big woman, Minnie can look so little and lost and lone and helpless sometimes, setting on a bar stool with nothing but a little glass of Scotch when what she really craves is a double, that almost any strange man will take pity on her and say, 'Baby, I beg your pardon, perhaps you would accept some refreshments on me.'

"If he makes a polite approach, Minnie will turn her head to one side, somewhat down, and reply, 'With utmost pleasure—if you introduced yourself. But I do not drink with no man I do not know.'

" 'My name is So-and-so-and-so,' says the stud.

"Whereupon, Minnie says her name is Minnette, and that she were a Johnson before her mother married her third stepfather. Then, says Minnie, she took the name of Ashmore. But sometimes Minnie forgets which stepfather's name she took—*Butler* or *Ashmore*—which makes no difference because by then she has ordered a double Scotch on the man and their friendship is cemented. Minnie do not spend another dime of her own money that evening. My Cousin Minnie has a way with men, Boyd. She makes chumps out of them so sweet-like. It might take a man several months to find out Minnie can be big, bad, bold, and boisterous if she wants to. If a man goes too far with Minnie, she can raise her voice and embarrass him proper. Ray Charles can be screaming on the TV and Bill Doggett yelling on the juke box both at once, but you can still hear Minnie in the bar above all that noise telling some old joker, 'Don't let your licker go to your head, daddy, because if you do, I'll blow you off your feet. You done barked up the wrong tree, insulting me. Bartender, tell this man to vacate my person.'

"But by that time it is nearly closing, and the man has spent all his money anyhow. If he makes no argument, Minnie will calm down and say real ladylike, as she rises to leave—alone—'Good night.'

"But if the man raises his voice and asserts his manhood, it is not good night that Minnie says to that cat as she goes out the door. Oh, no, it is not good night. It is a word that begins with a letter I do not like to mention. Minnie knows more bad words than I do. To tell the truth, sometimes I think my Cousin Minnie is a disgrace to the race."

"Why?" I asked.

"Because, in protecting her ladyhood, Minnie does not always act like a lady. I told you about the time she hit that man in the bar with a beer bottle New Year's Eve, did I not?"

"You did. So?"

"It would have been more politer—and cheaper, too— had Minnie hit him with something that did not contain good alcohol," said Simple. "Or if she had screamed and throwed a glass. But Minnie did not scream. She just up and knocked the man out with a bottle. Should not a lady settle things in a more gentler manner? Maybe even faint first?"

"Your concept of the word 'lady' evidently comes from remote romantic sources," I said. "Gentle ladies in the days of antiquity never had to face the problems Minnie has to face. In fact, the whole conventional concept of the word 'lady' is tied up with wealth, high standing, and a sheltered life for women. Minnie has to face the world everyday, in fact, do battle with it."

"True," said Simple, "to remain a lady, Minnie often has to fight. It is not always easy for a colored lady to keep her ladyhood."

"You are bringing up race again," I said. "But this time I think you put your finger on the crux of the argument."

"The crust of the argument is that Minnie believes in peace so much she will fight for it," said Simple. "When Minnie wants the right to be let alone, she means to *be let alone*. Yet she will lead a man on, let him spend his whole wages on Scotch, beer, or wine—it depending on how much wages he has got as to which class she puts him in. Then when the man wants to bother Minnie, she does not wish to be bothered. That is what leads to trouble. I have told my cousin that mens were not made to be taken advantage of. But ever since Eve, that is what womens have done. I reckon I cannot change Minnie."

"Men do not have to let women run away with their senses," I said.

"No," said Simple, "but they do. There was a time when a woman could twist me, as much sense as I got, around her little finger. In fact, at one time Zarita had me all balled up in her little tiny fist. But that were before I met Joyce, my wife, who now has got me tied to her apron strings."

"Not very tightly," I said, "as often as I see you here in Paddy's Bar."

"Before I got married, I used to be in here every night the Lord sent," said Simple. "Now I am only in here every other night—or so."

"Or so, is right," I said.

"But I do not drink like I once did," claimed Simple. "Neither do I stray. My eyes might roam, but I stay home. I have got a good home, pal, which I mean to keep. What I wish is that my Cousin Minnie would settle down and make herself a good marriage, too. Minnie has been in Harlem long enough to get the country out of her hair now, and Virginia out of her system. Yet Minnie is in this bar more often than me. She is getting to be a settled woman now, so she ought to settle down—and not on a bar stool neither. A lady should not hang out in places which are shady. I have told Minnie she is liable to get hurt sometimes, the way she does her boy friends. A man can put up with so much, but Minnie sometimes piles it on."

"From all you have told me about Minnie, she can protect herself," I said.

"At the expense of her ladyhood," said Simple. "A woman should not put herself in a position where she has to fight her way out."

"You never forced a woman into such a position yourself?" I asked.

"Being a man, naturally, I have sometimes tried to make my point—and over-made it," admitted Simple. "My first wife, Isabel, once attacked me so ferocious, the neighbors had to help me get out of the house. That were in Baltimore. Since I come to New York, I have got more sense. Yet there is some chumps in Harlem who take one look at any woman, including Minnie, and their senses desert them. What is it about womens that makes a man lose his mind?"

"You answer that, if you can."

"I reckon it must be their ladyhood," declared Simple.

COFFEE BREAK

"My boss is white," said Simple.

"Most bosses are," I said.

"And being white and curious, my boss keeps asking me just what does THE Negro want. Yesterday he tackled me during the coffee break, talking about THE Negro. He always says 'THE Negro,' as if there was not 50-11 different kinds of Negroes in the U.S.A.," complained Simple. "My boss says, 'Now that you-all have got the Civil Rights Bill and the Supreme Court, Adam Powell in Congress, Ralph Bunche in the United Nations, and Leontyne Price singing in the Metropolitan Opera, plus Dr. Martin Luther King getting the Nobel Prize, what more do you want? I am asking you, just what does THE Negro want?'

" 'I am not THE Negro,' I says. 'I am *me*.'

" 'Well,' says my boss, 'you represent THE Negro.'

" 'I do not,' I says. 'I represent my own self.'

" 'Ralph Bunche represents you, then,' says my boss, 'and Thurgood Marshall and Martin Luther King. Do they not?'

" 'I am proud to be represented by such men, if you say they represent me,' I said. 'But all them men you name are *way* up there, and they do not drink beer in my bar. I have never seen a single one of them mens on Lenox

Avenue in my natural life. So far as I know, they do not
even live in Harlem. I cannot find them in the telephone
book. They all got private numbers. But since you say
they represent THE Negro, why do you not ask them what
THE Negro wants?'

" 'I cannot get to them,' says my boss.

" 'Neither can I,' I says, 'so we both is in the same boat.'

" 'Well then, to come nearer home,' says my boss, 'Roy
Wilkins fights your battles, also James Farmer.'

" 'They do not drink in my bar, neither,' I said.

" 'Don't Wilkins and Farmer live in Harlem?' he asked.

" 'Not to my knowledge,' I said. 'And I bet they have
not been to the Apollo since Jackie Mabley cracked the
first joke.'

" 'I do not know him,' said my boss, 'but I see Nipsey
Russell and Bill Cosby on TV.'

" 'Jackie Mabley is no *him*,' I said. 'She is a *she*—better
known as Moms.'

" 'Oh,' said my boss.

" 'And Moms Mabley has a story on one of her records
about Little Cindy Ella and the magic slippers going to
the Junior Prom at Ole Miss which tells all about what
THE Negro wants."

" 'What's its conclusion?' asked my boss.

" 'When the clock strikes midnight, Little Cindy Ella is
dancing with the President of the Ku Klux Klan, says
Moms, but at the stroke of twelve, Cindy Ella turns back
to her natural self, black, and her blonde wig turns to a
stocking cap—and her trial comes up next week.'

" 'A symbolic tale,' says my boss, 'meaning, I take it,
that THE Negro is in jail. But you are not in jail.'

" 'That's what you think,' I said.

" 'Anyhow, you claim you are not THE Negro,' said my boss.

" 'I am not,' I said. 'I am *this* Negro.'

" 'Then what do *you* want?' asked my boss.

" 'To get out of jail,' I said.

" 'What jail?'

" 'The jail you got me in.'

" 'Me?' yells my boss. 'I have not got you in jail. Why, boy, I like you. I am a liberal. I voted for Kennedy. And this time for Johnson. I believe in integration. Now that you got it, though, what more do you want?'

" 'Reintegration,' I said.

" 'Meaning by that, what?'

" 'That you be integrated with *me*, not me with you.'

" 'Do you mean that I come and live in Harlem?' asked my boss. 'Never!'

" 'I live in Harlem,' I said.

" 'You are adjusted to it,' said my boss. 'But there is so much crime in Harlem.'

" 'There are no two-hundred-thousand-dollar bank robberies, though,' I said, 'of which there was three lately *elsewhere*—all done by white folks, and nary one in Harlem. The biggest and best crime is outside of Harlem. We never has no half-million-dollar jewelry robberies, no missing star sapphires. You better come uptown with me and reintegrate.'

" 'Negroes are the ones who want to be integrated,' said my boss.

" 'And white folks are the ones who do *not* want to be,' I said.

" 'Up to a point, we do,' said my boss.

" 'That is what THE Negro wants,' I said, 'to remove that *point*.'

" 'The coffee break is over,' said my boss."

LYNN CLARISSE

"How nice to be respectably dirty," said Simple's cousin, Lynn Clarisse, who had one of those double names like many girls, colored and noncolored, have down South. "How nice," she said "to be able to read *Another Country* and *The Carpetbaggers* and John Burroughs and Henry Miller and *The Messenger*, even *City of Night* and *Last Exit to Brooklyn* without blushing—because everybody else is reading them. There are lots of things in those books I know, of course, since I am full-grown and adult. But there are more things I don't know, at least not from experience."

"Let's experience a few," I said—testing her out, of course.

"We can't even get started on the spur of the moment, Mr. Boyd," she said, coming right back with an answer without blushing. No stammering. She wasn't a bit "country."

"You must have gone to a sophisticated college," I said. "Was it white, black, or integrated?"

"Fisk, as I know *you know* I told you," she said.

"Yes, you did," I remembered, "last night when Simple took me by his house to meet you. How come you have a cousin like Simple?"

"He's in the family," said Lynn Clarisse, "and is one

relative who happens to be down with it. I love that cat, and I love his Harlem."

"I do, too," I said. "He told me you were colleged. But I sort of expected a girl whose mind did not go beyond the classroom, you know, conventional."

"There are no limits to where the mind or body goes," said Lynn Clarisse. "My body has been on Freedom Rides. See that scar where an Alabama cop tried to break my neck with his billy club. He just broke my shoulder, but it left a scar on my neck where his club burst the skin open. It might sound pretentious to say it, but while my body was in Alabama that night, my mind was on Sartre and Genet."

"Are you really colored?" I asked, just playing, of course.

"Are you blind?" she replied. She laughed. I laughed. "I am darker than dark brownskin." But the mystery was not solved. She had never been North before, Lynn Clarisse. So, how come so suave, so bright, so—well?

"Maybe you don't know it," she said, "but we do have libraries in Nashville, too. Integrated just like New York. And Fisk, a colored college, you know, only slightly integrated, has one of the best libraries in the country, and a librarian who helps students choose good books. We have a browsing room where some can browse, and others can sleep, whisper sweet nothings, or just clean their fingernails—sort of nice place. As for reading books, even far-out books, even beatnik books, fine. Only there are not enough books for me down South, which is one reason I came to New York. Or maybe I came to see books in action. Slow motion, though, so don't rush me, Mr. Boyd."

"I'm too flabbergasted," I said. "I can't believe you are Jesse B. Semple's cousin."

"Flesh and blood," she replied. "And he brought me in this café, which is the nicest one, so he says, on 125th Street. You know he's up there at the bar, so if you still don't believe I'm his cousin, call him and ask him."

"Let's not bother Simple this moment," I said. "We're cozy back here in this booth. Say, Lynn Clarisse, have you seen any plays in New York?"

"Not yet."

"Could I take you to see some? What do you want to see?"

"Anything with my people in it," said Lynn Clarisse, "the Sammy Davis musical, Ruby Dee in Shakespeare, Gilbert Price, Diana Sands, a LeRoi Jones play if any are running, *Othello*."

"You are a race woman for true," I said.

"I've got to keep up with my own culture," said Lynn Clarisse. "Those plays will hardly be touring down South."

"I thought you were going to stay up North awhile?"

"A few weeks. Then I'm going back South. We've got things to do."

"More Freedom Rides?"

"Voter Registration."

"I'll miss you when you leave."

"Come down South," said Lynn Clarisse.

"We've got things to do in Harlem, too," I said.

"And me, I have got something to do right now," interrupted Simple at the edge of our booth. "I have got to go home."

"All married men should be home by midnight," I said, motioning him away.

"Also all young ladies who come out in the evening

with their cousins in Harlem," added Lynn Clarisse. "So good night, Mr. Boyd."

"You are both going and leave me all alone in this bar?" I asked.

"With 50-odd Negroes and the white proprietor, you'll have company," said Simple. "I will even order you a beer on me and drop a quarter in the juke box before I depart, so you can listen to Nina Simone. Good night, old boy."

"Good night, my erstwhile friend."

"Good night, Mr. Boyd," said Lynn Clarisse.

"Good night!"

INTERVIEW

"Sometimes the *New York Times* looks almost like the Harlem *Amsterdam News*," said Simple. "There is so much Negro news some days from front to back in the *Times* that it seems like a colored paper. My wife, Joyce, says she reads the *Times* because it contains all the news that is fit to print. But for me it do not have as many pictures as the *Daily News*. Also it is hard to make out in the *Times* what the winning number is. For them that places bets on the numbers each and every day, and several times a day, that is important. Now, I am not much of a gambling man myself. But practically all my neighbors plays the numbers."

"I thought numbers was illegal in New York," I said.

"Ha-ha! If it wasn't for the numbers, half the people in Harlem would be earning no spending change at all, and Adam Powell would never have got on the front pages of the papers for being sued over how they say he called that widow lady a bag-woman.

"If the *New York Times* would just print the lead numbers, also the final number up there on its front page in that top left-hand box underneath 'All the News That's Fit to Print,' that paper might outsell the *Daily News* in Harlem—because even in the *News* the numbers is hard to unscramble for them that do not know how. Numbers might as well be printed out plain in the New York papers. If playing numbers is a sin, since sin is so open, why should it be hidden? If a man can bet at the race track, or play bingo in church, why should he not play the numbers in the barbershop, in his car, or, if you are a lady, in your beauty shop or laundromat?"

"Folks do play numbers in all those places," I said, "so why ask unnecessary questions?"

"Just to make conversation," grinned Simple. "You know I like to talk."

"I know," I said. "But you used to talk about civil rights."

"Yes," said Simple. "So many statements have been made, so many words have been said, so many reports rendered, surveys surveyed, Freedom Rides rode, and speeches spoke, sit-ins sat, that I do not know what else to say that is polite. What I were to say now would not be fit to print."

"Do you expect to be quoted by the *Times?*" I laughed.

"Not hardly," said Simple. "My name is not Roy Wilkins, neither Rev. King. I am also not this famous writer whose name is Baldwin. And no white reporter has caught me on a Harlem corner yet to get a candid interview from me, just a man in the street, because I do not spend my time on corners. When white folks look in this bar and find it full of Negroes, they most in generally do not come in, not even to see me. So I have not been interviewed."

"Suppose you were caught some night on a corner and interviewed by a white reporter from a downtown paper, what would you say?"

"An interview means to express your views, does it not?"

"I think so," I said.

"Then would it not be better for a man to *view* my views, rather than just to hear my views?" asked Simple.

"Probably so," I said, "if visualization be possible."

"Then to that young white reporter I would say, 'Actions speak louder than words, so get down with the action, man.' I would tell him, 'Move to Harlem, man. At the same time, let me move downtown where you live. Change pads with me. You and your family take my apartment uptown, and let me and my family take your apartment downtown. Just for a month, we will swap places. Then after thirty days, you interview me and I will interview you. By that time you will have found out how much the difference is in the price of a pound of potatoes uptown and a pound of potatoes downtown, how much the difference is for what you pay for rent downtown and what I pay for rent uptown, how different cops look downtown from how cops look uptown, how much more often streets is cleaned downtown than they is uptown. All kinds of things you will see in Harlem, and not have to be told. After we swap pads, you would not need to interview me,' I would say, 'so let's change first and interview later.'"

"You would just be trying to make it hard for that young white reporter," I said. "You know he would have no time to make an investigation in depth of life in Harlem, so why not simply give him your summation in a few words?"

"I could do it in *one* word," said Simple, "but it would not be a word fit to print."

SIMPLY SIMPLE

"Almost nobody in this world ever does everything right," said Simple, "so everybody ought to have the right to do *some* things wrong—including Adam Powell. Powell is a Baptist. When I were a child in Virginia, the Baptists could do no wrong. Also, down South if you was *not* a Baptist, your soul were lost. Just to be sprinkled a Methodist, your soul was just not saved. You had to be dipped—with water in your ears Baptist-style—to be saved. When I were baptized, I was almost near drowned. That Sunday when I come up out of that holy water, the minister said, 'Jesse B. Semple, what have you to say?'

"I said, 'Reverend, you is trying to drown me.'

"Old Rev. said, 'Has the Spirit entered into your soul this morning?'

"I said, 'All I know is, I am full of water.'

"Rev. said, 'You are one of these hardened sinners. You must go and come again.'

"I went—but I have not been baptized again. But, since I have been having a toothache lately, I think I will be a Christian Scientist like my wife lately is. Joyce says a toothache is all mind."

"I thought you told me you loved gospel songs," I said. "There is no gospel singing in Christian Science churches."

"What?" asked Simple. "Then I will go to Bishop Child's temple where there is a fine choir. I was just trying to save dentist's bills and follow my wife's advice."

"Religion is designed to save your soul," I said, "not your teeth."

"Neither does religion help you on your income tax," said Simple. "Look at Adam Powell, pastor of the biggest Baptist church in the world, and they got him in the income-tax wringer. I asked Joyce what the Christian Scientists would say about that. Joyce said Science would say, 'Nothing is but thinking makes it so.'

"I said to my wife, 'If that be true, then what about our budget for food, house, and upkeep? Some weeks you tell me you cannot balance our budget unless I give you *all* my salary. Why don't you just *think* that I gave it all to you? Then our budget would be balanced and everything would be O.K.'

"Joyce said, 'Jess Semple,' and she shook her finger, 'don't be simple.'

"I said, 'Baby, don't shake your finger in my face. That is probably why Venus got her arms cut off—from shaking her fingers in some man's face once too often. And look at Mona Lisa smiling that sly little old smile, setting there thinking up ways to bedevil a man. I can tell by how she looks, Mona Lisa is up to no good purpose. If Mona Lisa was to come to life here in New York and take the A Train to Harlem, I would send her right back to France where she belongs. That woman would ruin a man—like Desdemona did Old Fellow."

"You mean Othello?" I said.

"Whoever that Negro were that was driv mad by a white handkerchief," said Simple.

"It was not Desdemona's fault," I explained. "It was Iago's."

"Whoever it were, Old Fellow had seen too many of them Mona Lisa smiles by that time to trust any woman," declared Simple. "Me, I trust nobody but my wife. She very seldom smiles. Joyce laughs—and when Joyce laughs, she's got a whole mouth full of teeth that flash like a house in the sea—I am telling you, man, I love to see Joyce laugh. But oh, my! When my wife gets mad, her eyes flash like lightning and her lips get thin as a buzz saw. That is when I leave the house and come here to the bar to get me a beer. Joyce never did smile no in-between smile like Mona Lisa."

"Did you go to the museum to see Mona Lisa?" I asked.

"I did not," said Simple, "but Joyce went and come back and told me what she looked like. I also seed Mona Lisa in all the papers. Even our Harlem *Amsterdam News* had her picture on the front page. That is why I thought Mona was colored. But my wife told me, no, she is not Afro-American, she is white. I might have knowed in that case a man dare not say, 'Hi, baby!' to her for fear he will be put out of the museum.

"Joyce asked me why would I want to say, 'Hi, baby!' to Mona Lisa.

"I said, 'Just to see if she would laugh.'

"Joyce said, 'It is very crude of a man to speak to a strange woman you do not know.'

"I said, 'If I paid a dollar to look at Mona Lisa in a museum, I should at least have the privilege of saying hello to her. Even if she did come from France, she is no more than any other woman displaying herself in public, except that Mona is in a frame and you do not see much more than her head. I would like to see how Mona is built, myself.'

" 'Mona Lisa is a work of art. Her face reveals her all,' said Joyce. 'That single detail of her smile speaks mysteries.'

" 'Miseries,' I said, 'also hell and damnation for whoever were her husband.'

" 'How do you know she had a husband?' said Joyce.

" 'The *Amsterdam News* says Mona were pregnant. And when a thing is in the papers,' I said, 'everybody believes it.'

" 'The papers do not know anything about the private life of Mona Lisa,' said Joyce. 'Neither does anybody else. What does her smile mean? Who knows?'

" 'Maybe she is listening to a record by Dick Gregory,' I said."

GOLDEN GATE

"If I was of mind to give a Christmas gift to the Devil," said Simple, leaning on the bar with an empty glass of beer, "I would give him Mississippi, the whole state of Mississippi, police dogs and all."

"You would be too generous with the Devil," I said, "giving him a whole state with all of those sinners in it to torture. He would have a lot of fun."

"I would not want the Devil to have fun with no present I gave him," said Simple. "No! So I better give something to bedevil him. Maybe I'd give him all the roughnecks in Harlem—garbage out the windows, pop bottles, and lighted cigarette butts. I would have the Devil hit on the head with a sack of garbage every time he switched down the streets of hell."

"I would go you one better. For Christmas I would turn the Devil black and let him find out what Jim Crow is like."

"Hell sure must be full of white folks," said Simple, "so if the Devil was black, he would be bound to have a hard time. Suppose he wanted to drive a train and be an engineer, the Railroad Brotherhoods in hell would not let him in the union. Suppose he wanted to get a cup of coffee driving on the highway between the Capital of hell and

Baltimore, he would have a hard time. Suppose he wanted to play golf in Alabama, he would be burnt up. To turn him black would be a *real* Un-Merry Christmas for the Devil. But since, I am not going to hell myself, why worry about it. I am wondering what it is gonna be like when I get to Glory. There must be white folks up there, too.

"You know," continued Simple. "Last night I drempt I died and went to heaven and Old Governor of Mississippi, Alabama, or Georgia, or wherever he is from, had got there before me, and didn't want to let me in. He was standing at the Golden Gate, right beside Saint Peter, when I come ghosting up.

"He said, 'What are you doing here, Jess Semple? Don't you know you have to use the rear entrance?'

" 'What rear entrance?' I says.

" 'The COLORED ENTRANCE,' says Old Governor, 'around the back.'

"I said, 'I did not know heaven was located in the South. I thought it was *up* not *down*. Saint Peter, do you hear the man?'

"Saint Peter said, 'Heaven is so full of white folks now I have no control over it any more.'

"I said, 'How did so many white folks get to heaven, Saint?'

"Old Peter said, 'Jesse B. Semple, I do not know, but they are here.'

" 'I did not realize I was in hell,' I said. 'I thought when I riz through space from my dying bed, I had landed at the Gate of Heaven. Anyway, Peter, is not my sins washed whiter than snow? Am I not white now inside and out?'

"Whereupon, Old Down-home Governor spoke up and said, 'You have to bathe in the River of Life to be washed whiter than snow. The River of Life is in heaven. You are not inside yet, Simple. Therefore, you are still black. White is right, black get back! You are not coming in the front entrance.'

"I said, 'It is too bad I left my weapons down on earth. I am not a Freedom Rider, neither a sit-in kid. The two cheeks I have to turn have done been turned enough. They shall turn no more. You-all better get out of my way and lemme through this Golden Gate.'

"Saint Peter begun to wring his hands. He said, 'I will go call Gabriel. He is one of your folks. He can explain to you how things is up here since the white folks took over.'

"I said, 'Call Gabriel, nothing. If you gonna call anybody, call God!'

" 'God is busy with Vietnam, West Berlin, and NATO,' said Peter.

" 'I did not know God's name was Uncle Sam,' I said. 'Besides, I am as much angel as you, Peter. If you and Old Gov. there don't get out of my way and let me in this gate, I will take my left wing and slap you both down. Then I will take my right wing and whip you good.'

" 'Jesse B., we go in for nonviolence in heaven,' cried Peter.

" 'I am not in heaven, yet,' says I, 'only on the threshold. But if I don't get in, it won't be because I didn't try. Where is Old Governor gone at?'

" 'He has run to call his dogs,' said Peter.

" 'You mean to tell me, you let Southern white folks and their dogs both in heaven,' I asked. 'What is the sky coming to? Earth were bad enough. Maybe the Lord sent for me to clean up heaven. In which case, wait a minute. I will ghost back to earth and round up my boys from Harlem. I will ask them are you willing to die for your rights in heaven as on earth? If so, *die now*, make ghosts out of the Golden Gate. White folks have done got up there and made an American out of Saint Peter. They have set up a kennel of police dogs beside the River Jordan. They have put up WHITE ONLY signs at the milk-and-honey counter. Mens, do you intend to stand for this? Whereupon, from their stepladders on every corner in Harlem they will answer, "No!" Peter, I'll bet this Golden Gate will open then. We'll see. We'll see!'

"Whiz-zzz-zz-z! But when I ghosted back to earth, I woke up kicking and sweating, and found out that it were nothing but a dream. I were not dead at all—just having nightmares in my sleep. It is a good thing, because had my dream been real, I would of tore up that Golden Gate! Plumb up! White folks can run hell, if they want to, but they better not start no stuff with me in Glory Land."

JUNKIES

"Something is always happening to a man, especially if he is colored," said Simple at the bar. "The next atom bomb is liable to fall on me. Of course, the good thing about the bomb is that it will fall on a whole lot of other people, too—some of who deserves to be annihilated. I am perfectly willing to go myself, if my enemies in Mississippi are taken along with me. 'Greater love hath no man than that he lay down his life to get even.'"

"Where did you get that quote?" I asked. "It's not in the Bible."

"I made it up myself," said Simple. "An eye for an eye, a wig for a wig, and a tooth for a tooth. When both eyes are gone, all teeth are knocked out, and all wigs snatched, then let the bomb fall."

"Are you trying to say you are in favor of atomic warfare?"

"Air-raid shelters would do no good," said Simple, "because when you come out, your favorite bar would be blowed to hell and gone, your best barbershop would be missing, and your pastor dead from passive resistance. Passive resistance is not for me. I say, if die you must, let's die going down with the action."

"You are a fascist, a Birchite, an extreme rightest," I said.

"Is I?" said Simple. "Since the Republican Party seems to be going extreme right these days, I think colored folks ought to go extreme black. Since one end is pro and the other end is con, if you try to pro-test and con-test in between, you is sure to get hit. I sees no point in being the middleman. If I am all them names you just called me for being on the black side, O.K.—you be what you want to be and let me be, too. And buy me a beer for the sake of our friendship. If the bomb falls, I will let you come in my bomb shelter."

"How kind of you," I said. "But I don't believe in violence on an international or national scale."

"Between the violent and the nonviolent," said Simple, "it looks like to me neither one of them will win in the U.S.A., because if there was to be a race war, how is twenty million Negroes going to fight two hundred million white folks? And if Negroes was to pray-in and kneel-in and sing-in from now till Doom's Day and the white folks did not want to give us our civil rights, what more nonviolence could we do to make them stop twisting freedom's arm? Pray how? Picket who? Boycott what? March where?"

"Get the ballot," I said, "and use it. Vote! Vote in the South where we would have more than the balance of power. Vote in larger numbers and more intelligently in the North. Put more Negro representatives in political positions."

"Buy me a beer," said Simple, holding up his empty glass, "and let me tell you about Cousin Minnie. She hit the numbers last week for $116 clear cash after she had paid off her runner for being honest and bringing her her money."

"I declare!" I exclaimed.

"Minnie will declare nothing when income-tax time

comes," said Simple. "It is a good thing Minnie is not
famous like Adam Powell, else the government would get
her. I would hate to be rich and famous, too."

"That's a remote eventuality," I said.

"A remote something," said Simple. "Almost as remote
as my beer—which is gone. You are not setting us up
tonight?"

"My bar money is low."

"Mine, too," sighed Simple. "My wife do not trust me
with more than cigarette change from one day to another.
And she allots nothing for beer. Joyce is a budget fiend.
She loves to keep it balanced, but she hides the scales.
Right now I needs a glass of cool keggie. Must I beggie?"

"Begging will do no good. I told you my funds are low."

"So you've got nothing to spend, and you won't spend
that," said Simple.

"Oh, well, one for the road," I said.

"Whilst I tell you what I heard, which is an amaze-
ment," said Simple. "Every time I see Minnie, that cousin
of mine has some new kind of tale to tell. Last night she
was telling me about a junkie, the son of her neighbors
next door. Minnie says that boy's mother is ashamed of
him—a fine young man what turned out to be a junkie
while still in his teen-age years. They are a respectable
hard-working couple, his father being in the Post Office,
and that boy is their only child. Minnie says they keep a
nice home. But it seems lately their son-boy has been
going from bad to worse on junk, using the hard stuff, and
stealing things out of the house to support his habit—anything he can sell or pawn—their Chinese vase, the clock
radio, the electric iron, the toaster, even to the bathroom
scales.

"His mother has been trying to hide all these happenings from his father, this being their only son. She did not want the old man to know he took dope. Whenever the son would steal something, if Mama could find the pawn tickets in his dresser drawer, she would go and get the stuff back before Papa missed it. Almost every other day she had to go and get Papa's electric razor out of pawn. This went on all last summer. But seems like now the boy's habit has been getting worse and worser. One fix a day does not do him no more, neither two. Seems like he needs more and more money to feed the pushers. Do you know, that first cold snap one day last week, what his mother caught him doing?"

"No," I said.

"She caught him rummaging in her closet taking out her fur coat—her one and only fur coat that her husband worked hard to pay for. It were not a mink, but it was a good coat, and her son was about to steal it."

"What did she do?" I asked.

"Begged and pleaded with him not to take it. But he said, 'Mama, I got to have some cash.'

"She gave him what little money she had. But he just looked at them three or four dollars and hung onto the coat. 'I got to have more than that, Mama. *I got to have more.*' He started to the door, furs in hand.

"She said, 'Son, please!' But he paid her no mind. She tried to snatch the coat back, but her son hung on. She struggled and tussled with him. And finally she started crying, with the tears running all down her face.

"The boy did not want to hurt her, so he stopped tussling and said, 'All right, Mama,' and hung the coat back in the closet. He went out in the kitchen whilst his mother sunk down in an armchair to dry her tears. While she was wiping her eyes, that boy come out of the kitchen with a clothesline, sneaked up behind his mama, threw that rope around her, and tied her up in the chair—with the hard knots behind her back so there was no way for her to get loose. He took the coat and disappeared, her one and only fur coat taken by her one and only son! When the husband come home from work, there was Mama all trussed up and tied in the chair. The secret was out. She had to tell him their son was on dope."

"How sad!" I said.

"How sad is right," agreed Simple. "Somebody needs to do something about junk and junkies. How would any woman like to be tied up and robbed by her own son? It is like one of them horror strips in the comic books—only it ain't comic."

"It's not comic," I said.

DOG DAYS

"Added to all the other worriations she has in her life," said Simple, "my Cousin Minnie has now got another dog here in Harlem."

"What kind of dog?" I asked.

"A French poodle," said Simple.

"How on earth did Minnie get a French poodle?"

"From some old white lady for whom Minnie did some day's work. That old lady's poodle had poodles, and one of them puppy poodles became so attached to Minnie that the old lady asked Minnie if she had anywhere to keep a dog—if so, she could have it.

"Minnie said, 'I got a six-room apartment,' which were the biggest lie ever told, because Minnie has hardly got a six-foot room. Anyhow, the lady gave her the dog, and Minnie brought it home, all clipped and shaved with neck ruffs and leg ruffs like French poodles has when they is barbered right. But now that its hair is growing out again, that poodle looks like any other old dirty white ragball of a dog to me."

"A French poodle is an aristocratic kind of dog," I said, "which needs to be taken care of in high style, washed weekly, and clipped by experts. I doubt if Minnie has the time or money to give that dog the kind of care it needs to show off its pedigree properly."

"You may doubt it, but I *know* it, she hasn't," said Simple. "Minnie has already sung that dog its theme song, 'I Can't Give You Anything But Love.' She is fond of that dog, God knows, but my cousin has no business with a animal. There are too many dogs in Harlem as it is. She should have left that dog out on Long Island where it could run and romp with its own kind. A French poodle has no more business in a furnished room than a polar bear has in hell. Minnie cannot even afford to buy it dog food, let alone keep it trimmed and clipped. Why, that dog was even perfumed when she got it."

"What does Minnie feed it?" I asked.

"Scraps," said Simple, "on which it seems to thrive. Fact is, it is getting fat."

"French poodles are not supposed to get fat. They should be dieted so as to keep their figures long, slim, and trim."

"This poodle will soon be big as Minnie, I expect," said Simple, "also as dark, if she do not give it a bath soon."

"Poor thing!" I said. "What did Minnie name the dog?"

"Jane," said Simple.

"Why?" I asked.

"Because when Minnie first got it, it being a female, Minnie was always saying, 'That Jane sure is cute.' So she just named her Jane. Now, me, myself, I would not like to have no dog have a person's name. I would have called it Little Bits or Fluff or Snowball or Frenchie or Snoodles, something like that. How many dogs do you reckon there is in Harlem?"

"Certainly thousands," I said, "all over the place."

"I thought Harlem was going to the dogs," said Simple. "Anyhow, there are more dogs in the United States than there are Negroes."

"I did not know that," I said. "Where did you get hold of such a piece of information?"

"From the World Almanac which my wife buys every year," said Simple. "There are only about twenty million Negroes in America. But the World Almanac states there are twenty-two million dogs. Do you believe they count dogs more careful than they count Negroes?"

"It is easier to keep track of dogs because each dog has to have a license," I said. "Therefore most of them are registered."

"Negroes do not have to have a license," said Simple, "so it is not so easy to count us. Neither do we belong to anybody. But I'll bet back in slavery time every Negro was counted, and if one head were missing, the bloodhounds were sent after him. I would hate to be a slave chased by a bloodhound. In fact, I read somewhere once where in them days a good bloodhound was worth more than a good Negro, because a bloodhound were trained to keep the Negroes in line. If a bloodhound bit a Negro, nothing were done to the dog. In fact, Negroes were supposed to be bit."

"You can come up with the strangest information," I said.

"White folks do the strangest things," said Simple. "Imagine training a dog to chase Negroes! The kind of dog I would like to get acquainted with, me, myself, is that kind that walks around with a licker flask tied under his chin over there in them Swiss mountains, and if you need it, he will give you a drink."

"Saint Bernards," I said.

"Them dogs are saints," said Simple, "bearing drinks. I would like to have me a big dog like that, a dog that would not yip-yap-yip, but bark, BARK, BARK—I mean a real bass bark. I would like a dog-dog, not a play-dog, you know, a boxer, or a collie, or a nice old flop-eared hound. Not no poodle nor nothing like that. Neither no Doberman pinscher, which is too nervous a dog for me. And my dog would not have to own no pedigree. I do not want no dog finer than myself. But I sure would have me a dog if Joyce would let me."

"Your wife doesn't care for dogs?" I asked.

"She do, but not in a New York apartment," said Simple. "Joyce claims a dog should have a yard to run in and romp in, and also she has no time to be taking a dog out to walk on no lease mornings before she goes to work and evenings when it is time to cook dinner. Joyce says she knows I would not get up in time to do so, and when I come in from work I would be too tired, which is right. I reckon the real place for a dog is in the country where he could find a dogwood tree, and not have to depend on no fireplug. And speaking of dogwood trees, it were beneath one that I first found love in dog days in Virginia one August when the church had a picnic and that girl's grandma let me eat out of her picnic basket—since she thought I was hanging around because I wanted chicken. But what I really wanted was that girl, so we snuck off to the edge of the ravine and I kissed her beneath a dogwood tree."

"Why do you bring that up?" I asked.

"To revive my remembrance," said Simple. "Dog days and dogwood—dog-gone! And the chicken were good, too!"

POSE-OUTS

"Sit-ins and such, picketings and such, for civil rights has been so common," said Simple, "that they no longer attracts attention. A lot of demonstrations nowadays do not even get in the papers any more. There has been too many, so I thought up something new."

"What?" I asked.

"Pose-ins," said Simple, "or pose-outs."

"What do you mean, 'pose-outs'?"

"Statues is often naked, are they not?" said Simple.

"Yes."

"Well, by pose-outs," said Simple, "I mean Negroes undressing down to their bare skin and posing naked as statues for freedom's sake. Twenty million Negroes taking off every stitch—stepping out of pants, dress, and drawers in public places and posing in the nude until civil rights have come to pass."

"You are demented," I declared.

"No," said Simple. "Nothing would attract as much attention to segregation, integration, desegregation, and ratiocination than if every Negro in this American country would just stand naked until Jim Crow goes."

"Fantastic!" I said. "Mad! Completely absurd!"

"Yes," said Simple, "at a certain time on a certain day

let even those Negroes that be in Congress—Dawson, Diggs, Adam Powell—like that first Adam in the Garden—rise naked to answer the roll call. Ordinary people, if at work in factories, foundries, offices, or homes, will establish a nude-in. If on the streets, a nude-out. Black waiters at the Union League Club, a nude-in. Colored boys pushing racks in the streets of the garment district, a nude-out. Black cooks could pose in white kitchens naked. Maids could pose dusting the parlor with nothing on but a dust cap. Pullman porters on trains in the raw. Redcaps at stations bare except for badge numbers. Ralph Bunche at the United Nations, naked as a bird. At home, a nude-in. On the street, a nude-out. Until all Negroes get our rights, we pose. You know that statue 'The Thinker'?"

"By Rodin," I said.

"Setting on a stone with nothing on in God's world— 'The Thinker'—with his chin in his hand, just setting lost in thought. Imagine James Farmer demonstrating for CORE at City Hall, posing at high noon naked, making like 'The Thinker,' chin in hand! Also on the same day at the same time Roy Wilkins upholding the NAACP, buck-naked between them two lions on the steps of the New York Public Library, with nothing on but his nose glasses. At the back of the library, on the terrace facing Bryant Park, Borough President Constance Baker Motley just as she came in this world, whilst at Fiftieth and Broadway where the theatres is, Miss Lena Horne, bare as Venus. Down the way a piece, in front of the Metropolitan Opera, Leontyne Price in all her glory on a podium, not a stitch to her name. The traffic tie-up on Broadway would be terrific. We would not need a stall-in. Nude-outs would be enough. In Central Park, Willie Mays, on Sugar Hill, Jackie Robinson. And uptown in Harlem at 125th and

Lenox I would place on a pedestal Miss Pearl Bailey."

"Unclothed?"

"Except by nature," said Simple. "With Negroes posing like statues all over town, traffic would jam. On Wall Street tickers would stop running. In Washington at the sight of Adam Powell in his birthday suit, filibusters would cease to be. In Atlanta, Rev. Martin Luther King, with not even a wrist watch on, would preach his Sunday-morning sermon. In New York colored subway conductors would report for duty in the all-together. Every waitress in Chock full o' Nuts would look like Eve before the Fall. In Harlem, Black Muslims would turn to Black Nudists. And at the Apollo, Jackie Mabley would break up the show. Oh, if every Negro in America, big and small, great and not so great, would just take his clothes off and keep them off for the sake of civil rights, America would be forced to scrutinize our cause."

"How shocking!" I said.

"Which is what we would mean it to be," declared Simple. "A nude-out to shock America into clothing us in the garments of equality, not the rags of segregation. And when Negroes got dressed again, we could vote in Mississippi."

"That would be when hell freezes over," I said. "Besides, by that time the Legion of Decency would have all of you in jail for indecent exposure."

"Not me," said SImple, "because I would be in Harlem. The colored cops in Harlem would be naked, too, so how would I know, without his uniform, that he were a cop?"

"Considering all the dangers involved, would you be the first to volunteer for a nude-out?" I asked.

"That honor I would leave you," said Simple.

SOUL FOOD

"Where is that pretty cousin of yours, Lynn Clarisse, these days?" I asked.

"She has moved to the Village," said Simple.

"Deserted Harlem? Gone looking for integration?"

"She wants to see if art is what it's painted," said Simple. "All the artists lives in Greenwich Village, white and colored, and the jazz peoples and the writers. Nobody but us lives in Harlem. If it wasn't for the Antheny Annie Arts Club, Joyce says Harlem would be a cultural desert."

"You mean the Anthenian Arts Club," I said.

"I do," said Simple. "But Joyce tells me that thirty years ago Harlem was blooming. Then Duke Ellington and everybody lived here. Books was writ all over the place, pictures painted, lindy hoppers hopping, jitterbugs jumping, a dance hall called the Savoy with fine big bands playing. No more! The only things Harlem is famous for now is Adam Powell, who seldom comes home, and the last riots. So Lynn Clarisse has moved to the Village. But we can always get on the subway and go down and fetch her."

"Or join her," I said.

"Or let her re-join me," said Simple. "Although I am not worried about Lynn Clarisse. She is colleged, like you,

and smart, and can take care of herself in the Village—
just like my Cousin Minnie can take care of herself in
Harlem. Every fish to his own water, I say, and the Devil
take them that cannot swim. Lynn Clarisse can swim, and
Minnie dead sure can float, whereas some folks can only
dog-paddle. Now me, my specialty is to walk on water. I
been treading on the sea of life all my life, and have not
sunk yet. I refuses to sink. In spite of womens, white folks,
landlords, landladies, cold waves, and riots, I am still
here. Corns, bunions, and bad feet in general do not get
me down. I intends to walk the water until dry land is in
sight."

"What land?"

"The Promised Land," said Simple, "the land in which
I, black as I am without one plea in my country 'tis of
thee, can be *me*. American the beautiful come to itself
again, where you can see by the dawn's early light what
so proudly we hailed as civil rights."

"The very thought makes you wax poetic, heh?"

"It do," said Simple. "But Joyce thinks Lynn Clarisse
should have moved to Park West Village, halfway between Harlem and downtown. Joyce thinks Greenwich
Village is a fast place where colored are likely to forget
race and marry white. My wife is opposed to intermarriage on the grounds of pride. Joyce says she is so proud
of her African heritage she don't want nobody to touch it.
But do you know what Lynn Clarisse says? She says,
'There is no color line in art.'

"My cousin and my wife was kind of cool to each one
another on the surface that day Lynn Clarisse moved out
of Harlem. But you know how easy womens get miffed
over little things. I don't pay them no mind myself. The
only thing that makes me mad is Cousin Minnie wanting

to borrow five dollars, which is always once too often. Lynn Clarisse do not borrow. She came to New York with her own money."

"Are her parents well off?"

"Her daddy, my first cousin on my half-brother's side, owns one of the biggest undertaking parlors in Virginia. He makes his money putting Negroes in segregated coffins in segregated graveyards. He sent Lynn Clarisse to college, and now has give her money for 'a cultural visit' to the North. Young Negroes used to have to struggle to get anything or go anywhere. Nowadays some of them have parents who have already struggled for them, so can help them get through college, and get up North, and get more cultured and live in Greenwich Village where rents is higher than they is in Harlem. Thank God, my cousin's daddy is an undertaker."

"Morticians and barbers are almost the only Negro businessmen whose incomes have not yet been affected by integration," I said. "Certainly, restaurants and hotels in Harlem have suffered. Banquets that once were held at the Theresa are now held at the Hilton and the Americana or the New Yorker. And the Urban League's annual Beaux Arts Ball is at the Waldorf. Negro society has taken almost all its functions downtown."

"But as long as white undertakers refuse to bury black bodies, and white barbers will not cut Negro hair, colored folks still have the burying and barbering business in the bag."

"Except that here in New York, I suppose you know, some wealthy Negroes are now being buried from fashionable downtown funeral homes."

"Where the mourners dare not holler out loud like they

do at funerals in Harlem," said Simple. "It is not polite to scream and carry on over coffins in front of white folks."

"Integration has its drawbacks," I said.

"It do," confirmed Simple. "You heard, didn't you, about that old colored lady in Washington who went downtown one day to a fine white restaurant to test out integration? Well, this old lady decided to see for herself if what she heard was true about these restaurants, and if white folks were really ready for democracy. So down on Pennsylvania Avenue she went and picked herself out this nice-looking used-to-be-all-white restaurant to go in and order herself a meal."

"Good for her," I said.

"But dig what happened when she set down," said Simple. "No trouble, everybody nice. When the white waiter come up to her table to take her order, the colored old lady says, 'Son, I'll have collard greens and ham hocks, if you please.'

" 'Sorry,' says the waiter. 'We don't have that on the menu.'

" 'Then how about black-eyed peas and pig tails?' says the old lady.

" 'That we don't have on the menu either,' says the white waiter.

" 'Then chitterlings,' says the old lady, 'just plain chitterlings.'

"The waiter said, 'Madam, I never heard of chitterlings.'

" 'Son,' said the old lady, 'ain't you got no kind of soul food at all?'

" 'Soul food? What is that?' asked the puzzled waiter.

" 'I knowed you-all wasn't ready for integration,' sighed

the old lady sadly as she rose and headed toward the door. 'I just knowed you white folks wasn't ready.' "

"Most ethnic groups have their own special dishes," I said. "If you want French food, you go to a French restaurant. For Hungarian, you go to Hungarian places, and so on."

"But this was an American place," said Simple, "and they did not have soul food."

"The term 'soul food' is still not generally used in the white world," I said, "and the dishes that fall within its category are seldom found yet in any but colored restaurants, you know that. There's a place where jazzmen eat across from the Metropole that has it, and one or two places down in the Village, but those are the only ones I know in Manhattan outside of Harlem."

"It is too bad white folks deny themselves that pleasure," said Simple, "because there is nothing better than good old-fashioned, down-home, Southern Negro cooking. And there is not too many restaurants in Harlem that has it, or if they do, they spoil everything with steam tables, cooking up their whole menu early in the morning, then letting it steam till it gets soggy all day. But when a Negro fries a pork chop *fresh*, or a chicken *fresh*, or a fish *fresh*, I am telling you, it sure is good. There is a fish joint on Lenox Avenue with two women in it that can sure cook fish. But they is so evil about selling it to you. How come some of these Harlem eating places hire such evil-acting people to wait on customers? Them two ladies in this fish place stand behind the counter and look at you like they dare you to 'boo' or ask for anything. They both look mad no sooner than you enter."

"I'll bet they are two sisters who own the place," I said. "Usually by the time Negroes get enough money to own anything, they are so old they are evil. Those women are probably just mad because at their age they have to wait on anybody."

"Then they should not be in business," said Simple.

"I agree," I said. "But on the other hand, suppose they or their husbands have been skimping and saving for years. At last, at the age of forty or fifty they get a little business. What do they want them to do? Give it up just because they have got to the crabby age and should be retiring, before they have anything to retire on?"

"Then please don't take out their age on me when I come in to order a piece of fish," said Simple. "Why them two ladies never ask you what you want politely. They don't, in fact, hardly ask you at all. Them womens looks at customers like they want to say, 'Get out of here!' Then maybe one of them will come up to you and stand and look over the counter.

"You say, 'Have you got any catfish?' She will say, 'No!' And will not say what other kind she has or has not got.

"So you say, 'How about buffalo?' She will say, 'We had that yesterday.'

"Then you will say, 'Well, what have you got today?'

"She will say, 'What do you want?' I have already said twice what I wanted that they did not have. So now I say, 'How about butterfish?'

"She says, 'Sandwich or dinner?'

"I say, 'Dinner.'

"She says, 'We don't sell dinners after ten P.M.'

" 'Then why did you ask me if I wanted a dinner?' says I.

"She says, 'I was paying no attention to the time.'

"I said, 'You was paying no attention to me neither, lady, and I'm a customer. Gimme two sandwiches.'

" 'I am not here to be bawled out by you,' she says. 'If it's sandwiches you want, just say so, and no side remarks.'

" 'Could I please have a cup of coffee?'

" 'We got Pepsis and Cokes.'

" 'A Pepsi.'

"She rummages in the cooler. 'The Pepsis is out.'

" 'A Coke.'

"She comes up with a bottle that is not cold. Meanwhile the fish is frying, and it smells good, but it takes a while to wait, so I say, 'Gimme a quarter to play the juke box.' Three records for a quarter.

"Don't you know that woman tells me, 'We is all out of quarters tonight.'

"So I say, trying to be friendly, 'I'll put in a dime and play just one then. What is your favorite record?'

"Old hussy says, 'There's nothing on there do I like, so just play for yourself.'

" 'Excuse me,' says I, 'I will play "Move to the Outskirts of Town," which is where I think you ought to be.'

" 'I wish my husband was here to hear your sass,' she says. 'Is your fish to eat here, or to go?'

" 'To go,' I says, 'because I am going before you bite my head off. What do I owe?'

" 'How much is two sandwiches to go?' she calls back to the other woman in the kitchen.

" 'Prices is gone up,' says the other hussy, 'so charge him eighty cents.'

" 'Eighty cents,' she says, 'and fifteen for the Pepsi.'

" 'I had a Coke,' I says.

" 'The same. You get a nickel change.'

" 'From a five-dollar bill?' I says.

" 'Oh, I did not notice you give me a five. Claybelle, have you got any change back there?'

" 'None.'

" 'Neither is I. Mister, you ought to have something smaller.'

" 'I do not carry small change around on payday,' says I. 'And what kind of restaurant is this, that can't even bust a five-dollar bill, neither change small change into a quarter for the record player? Don't you-all have nothing in the cash register? If you don't, no wonder, the way you treat a customer! Just gimme my five back and keep your fish.'

" 'Lemme look down in my stocking and see what I got there,' she says. And do you know, that woman went down in her stocking and pulled out enough money to buy Harry Belafonte. But she did not have a nickel change.

"So I said, 'Girl, you just keep that nickel for a tip.'

"If that woman owns the place, she ought to sell it. If she just works there, she ought to be fired. If she is the owner's girl friend, was she mine I would beat her behind, else feed her fish until a bone got stuck in her throat. I wonder how come some Harlem places have such evil help, especially in restaurants. Hateful help can spoil even soul food. Dear God, I pray, please change the hearts of hateful help!"

FLAY OR PRAY?

"Tooth by tooth, before you can turn around, it is gone," said Simple sadly, leaning on the bar.

"What *it?*" I asked.

"Your youth-hood," said Simple. "With some mens, time goes hair by hair. I hope I never get bald-headed and toothless *both*."

"You probably will in due time," I said.

"Everytime the dentist pulls a tooth, ten years is gone," said Simple.

"That is hardly true," I said. "The average man has 32 teeth in his head. Ten times 32 equals 320 and nobody has that many years to live. Besides, some people keep all of their teeth until they die."

"Some live snaggled-toothed," said Simple. "And others keep just enough teeth to get in the way of a new plate."

"They are foolish," I said. "Bad teeth in the head are a health hazard and they ought to come out."

"There are plenty of things in a man's head that ought to come out," declared Simple, "like evil thoughts, and imaging you is more than you is and getting stuck-up and important. Also prejudice should come out."

"You can't pull prejudice out of a man's head like you can teeth. No dentist living can do that."

(118)

"Rev. Martin Luther King tries to pray prejudice out, but sometimes I think we are gonna have to flay it out," said Simple.

"Violence never solved anything," I contended. "You can't physically beat attitudes, racial or otherwise, out of people's heads. Deep-seated fixations are a matter for the psychiatrists and psychologists, not bully boys with clubs."

"Many a Negro's head has been flayed by a billy club, and many black souls on the way to the polls have been stopped by a cop who said, 'Stay away! Don't vote today!' Then the Negroes go back home, their minds changed about the ballot. Clubs have changed many Negroes' minds down South. How come they can't change white minds?"

"Brute force never changed any Negro minds at all. Negroes still hold the same thoughts silently in the face of intimidation. They just don't exercise their prerogatives."

"In other words, they don't vote in Mississippi. They are scared to vote. But it looks like to me," said Simple, "as many Negroes as there are in Mississippi, they would make the white folks scared to try to make so many Negroes scared. If all them down-home colored folks was to rise up in one mass, imagine!"

"You don't believe in Rev. King's policies of nonviolence, I gather."

"Only for the nonviolent," said Simple. "If I lived down South, I would lose my temper."

"Then you would lose your head," I said.

"I am afraid I would," said Simple. "I have been up here in the free North too long to go down to the unfree South. But I will contribute money."

"Sideline fighter," I said. "Talker at the big gate! Advocate of violence against your white brothers!"

"White brothers? The closest I could ever come to a white relative would be a twenty-second cousin on my Indian grandmother's side," said Simple.

"Your Indian grandmother?"

"Yes, they said in our family that grandma was descended from Pocahuntas. And Pocahuntas were married to Captain John Smith—and Smith were white."

"So?"

"So that would make his white brother's children's great-grandchildren my twenty-second cousins. But relatives or not, I would raise my hand against them, was them white cousins to segregate me."

"Flay, I take it would be your attitude, rather than pray."

"I have already prayed," said Simple.

NOT COLORED

"That man was too evil to be human," mumbled Simple, "both of them."

"What man?" I asked.

"That man in the back of my mind, my third cousin, Tyson."

"I never heard of Tyson before. Is he another of your numerous relatives?"

"Tyson were too mean to buy his baby milk when his wife's breasts went dry," said Simple.

"And the other man you are talking about?"

"No relation. The other man were white and evil in a different kind of way—very nice to white folks, but evil to Negroes. It looked like his face would change from one mask to another when he seed a colored person."

"Did that man's path ever cross yours?" I asked.

"That is how come I thought about him," said Simple, "since I got a letter from my niece, Brendaleen. Brendaleen writ that that white man is still living right there in Virginia in the town where I were born but, thank God, not reared. Had that old man's paths and mine ever crossed after I got grown, I might of kilt him, I do believe. I know I sure would have been bound to kick him in his shins, like he kicked me once in mine. I were nothing but a child then, ten-eleven years old, going down the street by myself bouncing a ball, you know, like kids do. Right in front of the man Winclift's house, my ball bounced too high and landed up in a limb of his lilac bush at one corner of his front lawn. His lawn were green and pretty and his lilac bush smelt good and his house were beautiful and white with a fine veranda. Nothing like that house on the colored side of town. I liked to bounce my ball down that pretty street. But not no more, after it landed in his lilac bush—because when I went across a little tiny corner of his grass to reach up in that bush and get my ball, he yelled at me, 'Get off my lawn, boy!'

"I said, 'Yes, sir, soon as I get my ball.'

"With that he come running off his veranda like a charging bull, hollering like mad, 'Soon as *what* did you say?'

"I said, 'Soon as I get my ball,' and I did not move.

"That is when that grown white man hauled off and kicked me in my shins, not just one time, but twice, once on each one of my legs. Wow! You know how bad it hurts to get kicked on your shins? It hurted me so bad I could not cry and I could not run. So I just fell down and rolled myself off that grass onto the sidewalk. Then I sat up and reached down and held my legs until I could get up and walk away—without my ball.

"He said, 'I guess that will teach you little black bastards to get on my grass.'

"I did not say nothing. But then it was that tears come in my eyes, and they were not from bruises on my shins. When I got home and told the old folks about it, they just said Mr. Winclift were the meanest *young* white man in town. Now he is old, an old white man who I regret is not dead. I reckon he is just too mean to die. How come

Brendaleen to mention him in her letter is that she says he just last week hauled off and slapped his colored cook for, as he claimed, burning up a pan of biscuit bread. This colored cook-lady went and got a warrant out for him. But you know and I know, nothing will come of a warrant in that little old Southern town. She will just stay slapped, that's all, like I stayed kicked. Which is one reason why them Japanese do not want no parts of Americans in their hearts. They remember Hiroshima."

"You can certainly make some unconnected circles in a conversation," I said. "That is what I call a *non sequitur* for true."

"Don't you see no connection between atom-bomb-dropping in Japan and shin-kicking in Virginia?" asked Simple.

"No direct connection," I said.

"Then you are not colored," said Simple.

CRACKER PRAYER

"Well," said Simple, "this other old cracker down in Virginia who acted like Mr. Winclift what kicked my shins, one night he were down on his knees praying. Since he were getting right ageable, he wanted to be straight with God before he departed this life and headed for the Kingdom. So he lifted his voice and said, 'Oh, Lord, help me to get right, do right, be right, and die right before I ascends to Thy sight. Help me to make my peace with Nigras, Lord, because I have hated them all my life. If I do not go to heaven, Lord, I certainly do not want to go to hell with all them Nigras down there waiting to meet me. I hear the Devil is in league with Nigras, and if the Devil associates with Nigras, he must be a Yankee who would not give me protection. Lord, take me to Thy Kingdom where I will not have to associate with a hell full of Nigras. Do You hear me, Lord?'

"The Lord answered and said, 'I hearest thee, Colonel Cushenberry. What else wilst thou have of me?'

"The old cracker prayed on, 'Lord, Lord, dear Lord, since I did not have a nice old colored mammy in my childhood, give me one in heaven, Lord. My family were too poor to afford a black mammy for any of my father's eight children. I were mammyless as a child. Give me a mammy in heaven, Lord. Also a nice old Nigress to polish my golden slippers and keep the dust off of my wings. But, Lord, if there be educated Nigras in heaven, keep them out of my sight. The only thing I hate worse than an educated Nigra is an integrated one. Do not let me meet no New York Nigras in heaven, Lord, nor none what ever flirted with the NAACP or Eleanor Roosevelt. As You is my Father, Lord, lead me not into black pastures, but deliver me from integration, for Thine is the power to make all men as white as snow. But I would still know a Nigra even though he were white, by the way he sings, also by certain other characteristics which I will not go into now because a prayer is no place to explain everything. But You understand as well as I do, Lord, why a Nigra is something special.

" 'Lord, could I ask You one question? Did You make Nigras just to bedevil white folks? Was they put here on earth to be a trial and tribulation to the South? Did You create the NAACP to add fire to brimstone? You know, Lord, as soon as a Nigra gets an inch he wants an el. Give him an el, and he wants it ALL. Pretty soon a white man will not be able to sing "Come to Jesus" without a Nigra wanting to sing along with him. And you know Nigras can outsing us, Lord.

" 'Lord, You know I think it would be a good idea if You would send Christ down to earth again. It is about time for the Second Coming, because I don't believe Christ knows what Nigras is up to in this modern day and age. They is up to devilment, Lord—riding in the same train coaches with us, setting beside us on busses, sending their little Nigra children to school with our little white children. Even talking about they do not like to be segregated in jail no more—that a jail is a public place for which they also pay taxes.

" 'Lord, separate the black taxes from the white taxes, black sheep from white sheep, and Nigra soldiers from white soldiers before the next war comes around. I do not want my grandson atomized with no Nigra. Lord, dispatch Christ down here before it is too late. Great Lord God, Jehovah, Father, send Your Only Begotten Son in a Cloud of Fire to straighten out this world again and put Nigras back in their places before that last trumpet sounds. When I get ready to go to Glory, Lord, and put on my white robe and prepare to step into Thy chariot, I do not want no Nigras lined up telling me the Supreme Court has decreed integrated seats in the Celestial Chariot, too. If I hear tell of such, Lord, I elect to stay right here on earth where at least Faubus is on my side.' "

RUDE AWAKENING

"I don't know why I keep on dreaming so much here of late," said Simple, "but I reckon it is because it dreams so good to imagine again in my sleep that I am the ruler of Dixie, me, colored and all my people, in charge of the state we Negroes helped to make so beautiful. It is beautiful in Virginia—and me setting on the wide veranda of my big old mansion with its white pillars, the living room just full of chandeliers, and a whole slew of white servants to wait on me, master of all I surveys, and black as I can be! Oh, it is fine! And dear old Mammy Faubus what raised me, bringing me my mint juleps in the cool of the evening on a silver tray. You Yankee Negroes up North don't know what you missed by never having a dear old white Mammy.

"The other day whilst I was setting fanning in my cane-bottomed rocker on my white veranda, who should come bowing around the corner of the yard but my dear old Mammy Faubus, shading her old blue eyes from the sun with her wrinkled white hand. She said, 'Mister Semple, sir, might I trouble to ask you to do me and mine a mite of Christian favor?'

"I said, 'What is it, Mammy Faubus?'

"She said, 'Excuse me, sir, but a friend of mine from

that little old Caucasian Christian Church down in Buckra Town has come to the kitchen door to ask us white servants for donations to her Organ Fund. We gave her what dimes and quarters we poor souls had. But she says she knows the Lawd would bless her if she could just speak to a rich Negro like you, Mister Semple. Do you reckon you could let that poor old sister just come around here to the front porch and tell you, "Howdy"?'

" 'Send her around here, Mammy Faubus, but tell her to be careful not to tread on my petunias.'

" 'Thank you, Mister Semple.'

"Around the corner of the house came a dear old white mammy who right away I know I knowed, because she had raised colored Colonel Washington's oldest boy. I said, 'Why good evening, Mammy Eastland.'

"You would of thought that old white sister was about to grin her head off. 'Good evening, God bless you!' she says. 'And thank you for letting me come into your presence. Mister Semple, you are a fine colored man!'

" 'Try to help all you white folks wherever I can,' I said, 'especially when you are a friend of Mammy Faubus, what nursed me. What can I do for you, Mammy Eastland?'

" 'I am begging for my church,' she said.

"Poor old soul, I thought, with hardly a rag to her back, yet begging for the Lord! White folks is truly religious! I were so moved I got up out of my rocker, reached down in my pants pocket, and give her a dollar. 'Take that, Mammy Eastland,' I said, 'and God bless you in your work. Are you still with my friend Colonel Washington?'

" 'I would not leave them good Negroes for nothing,' shouted Mammy Eastland. 'Him and his family are next to God in my book. Just like you and your family folks, quality folks! God never made better Negroes! Thank you, Mister Semple, thank you!'

" 'Just don't let me hear about none of your grandchildren trying to get into our colored schools, Mammy Eastland. And tell that educated son of yours to stop working with the NAAWP because it don't mean you white folks no good. I have no respect for uppity young crackers—talking about writing President Adam Powell at his Summer White House about how bad conditions is here in the South. You *old* crackers know your place. I believe in respect where respect is due. If your son asks you who I respects, tell him his mammy.'

" 'You's too kind, Mister Semple!'

" 'Not a-tall,' I said, waving her away with a wave of my black hand. 'Get on down the road to your work, Mammy Eastland, back to Colonel Washington's house, and don't spend more than half of that church dollar for snuff.'

" 'Lawd, Mister Semple!' she laughed, whaw-whawing till her old white shoulders shook. To tell the truth, I thought she was going to crack up at my little snuff joke. That Mammy Eastland! Oh, well, no white folks, no fun! But I don't mind helping poor white folks a little. And I never was a man to brag about what I do for others. Neither do I boast about what riches I possess. Some folks I know is too notoriety.

"Seems like since colored folks have taken over in the South all a lot of Negroes like to do is boast about their white mammies. It is beginning to be tiresome. Every time a bunch of colored society folks gather for a bridge game, or a planter's punch, or plantation brunch, somebody has got to brag about their old white mammy. To tell the truth, I do not believe every Negro that says he had a white mammy, had one. But me, of course, I was raised by Mammy Faubus. And colored Colonel Washington always had Mammy Eastland in his family for years. But we is aristocrats. Some of these other Negroes is new come by wealth, but the Semples and the Washingtons have had money so long we ignore it. That explains why my old white mansion is somewhat run-down—I am just too rich to have it fixed—but the tradition is still there.

"Just last week I give Mammy Faubus the money for a new dress. Now I could not see Mammy Faubus go without some new clothes to wear to the barbecue she tells me her church is giving next week, after which there is going to be a big camp meeting and singing. I just love to hear white folks sing!

"But I cannot understand their cracker children, neither their grandchildren. Not knee high to a duck, some of these little blue-eyed crackerninnies, yet they got the nerve to want to go to our colored schools! What is getting into white folks since Chief Justice Thurgood Marshall handed down that last decree from the Supreme Court bench granting everybody the right to file another suit to get their rights? Don't they want to go through the orderly process of the courts and sue and file until they get to be old men and womens?

"If at first you don't succeed, file and file again, I say. White folks, these things take time. Don't rush into integration without preparation. Just because a handful of old Negroes wearing robes in the Supreme Court says your rights are constitutional, it does not mean they are institutional. Our great institutions like the University of Jefferson Lee belong to us, and not even with all deliberate speed do we intend to constitutionalize the institutionalization of our institutions. In the dear and simple words of Mammy Faubus, 'Let things stay like they is.' Go slow on the status quo. Just stop to realize how folks like Mammy Faubus would suffer if times was to change. Who would she work for?

" 'Mister Jesse B., your family always was quality Nigras,' says Mammy Faubus, her old blue eyes flashing with pride. 'And I sure is a lucky white woman to be working for you-all all these years,' she tells me every day.

" 'The reward for service is more service,' I told her. 'You can serve us till you die, Mammy Faubus. Never will you want for a pot of victuals in Mister Semple's kitchen.'

" 'But it do look like,' says Mammy Faubus, 'since you Nigras taken over the South, the price of collard greens is doubled and grits gone sky-high.'

" 'That is because you white folks do not like to work like you ought to,' I said, 'and your white young upstarts wasting their time setting at counters downtown where they will never get served as long as I am black. Mammy Faubus, can't you talk to your grandchildren?'

" 'This is a headstrong generation, Mister Semple, white or black. Won't listen to reason! Colored Judge Johnson last week didn't fine them white sit-iners but five dollars, then give them a chance to pay they fines. But, no! Them young white varmints said they had ruther set in jail until they can eat in them fine black barbecue joints where white folks never been known to eat before. Why, when I were young . . .'

" 'I know, Mammy Faubus, when you was young things was different. But times do change. Now white folks all want to be black. You wouldn't want to be black, would you, Mammy Faubus?'

" 'Not in the Kingdom!' cried Mammy Faubus. 'All I

want to do is save my soul. Let the Nigras take this world, just gimme Jesus!'

" 'Bless your sweet soul, Mammy Faubus!' I said. 'Bless your dear white soul! Now get back to your work. When you go out to the kitchen, fix me a fresh julep and slice off a few slices of that Smithfield ham with a biscuit to hold me till dinner. Fetch me my palm-leaf fan. It's right hot on this veranda today. After my snack I might just take a little nap, so hand me my footstool.'

"I did fall into a doze. But do you know," said Simple, "as soon as I went to sleep, I woke up—and found out it was all a dream. I mean I woke up for real. Negroes had not taken over the South. All I heard outside my window, which I drempt was a veranda, was them New York garbage trucks going by and the busses rumbling down Lenox Avenue.

"Some joker in the street was yelling, 'Hey, girl, wait for me!'

"And the girl yelled back, 'I can't wait! I'm late to work now!'

"It were daybreak in Harlem, and I woke up to the same old nightmare."

MISS BOSS

"They pass like shadows," said Minnie. "Men, they pass like shadows in and out of a woman's life. Men pass like shadows. And the man I have got right now is about to go because I am going to put him out!"

"Cousin Minnie," said Simple, "the trouble with you is, you like to rule. You like, in the end, to *put an end* to all your men. As long as I have known you, it is *you* who always ends things when the ending time comes."

"I pay the rent on my place—with *his* money, naturally, if I can get it. I close the door to my place when the dough don't come no more. I change the lock when I can no longer stand his face—and his contribution to the pot is a disgrace. I rule! Yes, you right, I rule."

"That is the trouble, Miss Minnie. You rules. But a man should rule. When you get ageable, Minnie, you are going to be all by yourself. Why don't you find a good man and get married and give him the keys to your heart?"

"I don't believe the keys to my heart has been filed to fit my lock yet. They ain't made. If they is, no man has them."

"You are selfish, Miss Minnie. You got them keys to your heart in your drawer and you won't give them to nobody. Trouble with you is, you wants to domineer all the time. To *boss*, to have the *last* lick, and the *last* word. You is no fit mate for a man who wants a helpmeet. I tell you now, you want to share, but not care. It is a wonder some man has not blowed you down before now with a pistol, out of pure aggravation. You are my cousin, it is true, Minnie, but I would not fall in love with you. And if I had a good buddy who was to look upon you with a loving eye, I would tell him, 'No, don't—because she won't.'"

"Whatsoever you might tell your friend," said Minnie, "would do no good if I wanted him for mine. What I want, I get. Jess Semple, you know I got a way with men."

"It is a bad way," said Simple. "For the mens involved, bad. You are like a spider with a web—a long-term operator—in which operation I would hate to be your fly."

"You just do not go for my type," said Minnie. "Some men like to be taken. Some men is the kind of mules you can drive to water—*and they drink*. Oh, my, my, my! The shadows of the mules that I have driv to water—driv to the creek of love!"

"And then hauled off and hit them on the haunches with a singletree," said Simple. "Minnie, you is a bad mule driver. I myself have seen you aggravate and upset several mens since I been knowing you here in Harlem, married and single mens. You is no respecter of persons when it comes to pants. How you do it—and get away with it—I do not know. You is no Lena Horne, no picture in a frame, no New Year's advertising calendar with a pretty mama's photo over JANUARY. No, Minnie—yet and still, you make your way."

"I do not do too much talking with a man," says Minnie, "I let him jive."

"Yes, and when he gets through, he come out more dead than alive. You, Minnie, goes in for long-time action."

"Right now, I have nobody," said Minnie. "I am alone. My last and latest shadow has done passed. Down the steps and out my downstairs door, down the street and around the corner, Henry has gone his way. All them nights we was together, now I say, 'Baby, call it a day!' What few clothes he left behind, I have put them in the cleaners and sent him the ticket by mail. Henry departed."

"You first met him in this bar, did you not?"

"No, I met him in the Green Beacon. He followed me here. I met that other one, Luther, in the Green Beacon, too. Facts is, I met several good men in that bar—where you do not hang out."

"I never interferes with your 'Good evenings' to nobody, Minnie, even if you is my cousin."

"No, but the men see you, my cousin, around and they are afraid to come on strong—like asking me where do I live and if they can come home with me. They see you and get all formal, Jess. That is why sometimes I set at the opposite end of the bar from all relatives. And I do not like to be lectured, so just leave me be. Shut up."

"I will, Miss Boss, I will."

"Thank you," said Miss Minnie.

DR. SIDESADDLE

Dear Dr. Sidesaddle:

I, Jesse B. Semple, better known as Simple, take pen in hand to write you this letter. I have just read your article in *See-Saw Magazine* in which you writ about how you and your family have completely integrated, and that you-all have no problems whatsoever with your white neighbors and your white friends in your white house in your white neighborhood in the sideskirts of White Manors. First, Dr. Sidesaddle, I want to ask you how you can say yours is a white neighborhood if you are there? If one drop of black blood makes a white man black, you *colored* being in a white neighborhood must do something to that neighborhood that is not white.

Anyhow, dear Dr. Sidesaddle, your office is here in Harlem where I live. All of your patients is colored. You know that Harlem is not integrated and neither am I. But if you was to invite me up to your house in the suburbans, it would give me a chance to see what integration is like. But, of course, if I was to come up there, I expect no sooner had I arrived than somebody would say there was one Negro too many in the neighborhood. Of all the pictures I saw of you and your surroundings in that colored

magazine last week, you and your wife and your children
was the only colored in the pictures. All your friends and
next-door neighbors are white.

The church you are going to in the pictures is white. I
saw you and your wife setting in this pew. In front of you
was white and behind you was white, and the minister
was white. I did not even see a Negro in the choir—and
you know Negroes can sing. Can't they have more than
just two Negroes—you-all—in a integrated church? And
when your children go to Sunday School do they ever see
a black angel on their Sunday School cards? Do you-all
ever sing any gospel songs? It looks like to me to be the
kind of church in which a tambourine is never shook.

I went to a integrated church once with my wife, Joyce,
downtown in New York City, in which, Joyce said, the
members are all looking for the higher things. The minister read his sermon off of a paper, and I must say it was all
I could do to keep from going to sleep. Nobody in the
congregation even said, "Amen!" When the songs were
sung, nobody clapped a hand. Joyce said, "This is a digni-
fied church."

I said, "It is dull to me."

Joyce said, "You do not appreciate thoughts in religion.
You want emotions."

I said, "I want something to keep me awake."

Dear Dr. Sidesaddle, in a integrated church does a
minister *have* to *read* his sermon? Or do all white ministers read from a paper? How come they are not so full of
the spirit that they can just spill out God's word without
first writing it down and reading it from a paper? They
just drone along and never raise their voices, even to say,
"Hallelujah!" I do not see how they ever make converts.
Was you converted in that white church, or did you just

integrate on general principles? I bet you do not even dare to pat your foot during a song.

In the pictures in that magazine, it shows you and your family being served your dinner by a Japanese butler. Now, dear Dr. Sidesaddle, I has nothing against the Japanese. But as bad as Negroes need work, why not me for your butler? And, since I expect you grew up on collard greens and ham, I do not think you was eating Japanese food. But what I am trying to get at—and to which I expects from you an answer—is this: As you roll down here to Harlem every day to your office in your white Thunderbird to give out prescriptions to black patients and operate on black appendages, then drive home every night to your white house in your white neighborhood in the suburbans, do you draw the color line yourself? Or is it your intention to integrate me along with you up there in White Manors someday? Dear Dr. Saddleside—I mean, Sidesaddle—that is all I wants to know as I sign off—

Yours sincerely truly,
Jesse B. Semple

WIGS FOR FREEDOM

"You ought to of heard my Cousin Minnie last night tell-ing about her part in the riots," said Simple, leaning on one of the unbroken bars on Lenox Avenue that summer, beer in hand. "After hearing three rebroadcasts of Mayor Wagner's speech after he flew back home from Europe, Minnie was so mad she wanted to start rioting again. She said old Wagner did not say one constructive thing. Any-how, Minnie come in the bar with a big patch on the top of her head, otherwise she was O.K., talking about all the big excitement and how she was in the very middle of it.

"Cousin Minnie told me, 'Just as I was about to hit a cop, a bottle from on high hit me.' Then she described what happened to her.

" 'They taken me to Harlem Hospital and stitched up my head, which is O.K. now and thinking better than before,' Minnie said. 'But, you know, them first-aid doc-tors and nurses or somebody in Harlem Hospital took my forty-dollar wig and I have not seen it since. I went back to Harlem Hospital after the riots and asked for my wig, an orange-brown chestnut blonde for which I paid cash money. But they said it were not in the Lost and Found. They said my wig had blood on it, anyhow, so it got throwed away.

" 'I told them peoples in the Emergency Room, "Not just my wig, but my head had blood on it, too. I am glad you did not throw my head away." Whereupon one of them young doctors had the nerve to say, "Don't sass me!" But since he was colored, I did not cuss him out.

" 'I knowed that young doctor had been under a strain —so many busted heads to fix up—so I just let his remarks pass. All I said was, "I wish I had back my wig. That were a real-hair wig dyed to match my complexion and styled to compliment my cheekbones." Only thing I regret about them riots is, had it not been for me wanting to get even with white folks, I would still have my wig. My advice to all womens taking part in riots is to leave their wigs at home.'

"I said, 'Miss Minnie, you look good with your natural hair, African style. I did not like you with that blonde wig on, nohow. Fact is, I did not hardly know you the first time I run into you on 125th Street under that wig. Now you look natural again.'

" 'The reason I bought that wig is, I do not want to look natural,' said Miss Minnie. 'What woman wants to look her natural self? That is why powder and rouge and wigs is made, to make a woman look like Elizabeth Taylor or Lena Horne—and them stars do not look like natural-born womens at all. I paid forty dollars for my wig just to look *unnatural*. It were *fine* hair, too! All wigs should always be saved in hospitals, bloody or not, and given back to the patients after their heads is sewed up. Since I were unconscious from being hit with a bottle, also grief-stricken from little Jimmy Powell's pistol funeral, when they ambulancetized me and laid me out in the hospital, I did not even know they had taken my wig off.'

" 'Do you reckon you will be left with a scar in the top of your head?' I asked.

" 'If I do,' said Miss Minnie, 'I am proud of it. What is one little scar in the fight for freedom when some people lose their life? Medgar Evers lost his life in Mississippi. All I lost was my wig in Harlem Hospital. And I know that cop did not hit me. He was busy hitting somebody else when I started to hit him; he didn't see me. Some Negro on a roof aimed a bottle at that cop's head—but hit me by accident instead. Bullets, billy clubs, and bottles was flying every whichaway that Sunday night after that Powell boy's funeral. Lenox Avenue were a *sweet* battle-ground. But I would not have been in action myself had not I seen a cop hit an old man old enough to be his father. He were a young white cop and the man was an old black man who did not do nothing except not move fast enough when that cop spoke. That young cop whaled him. WHAM! WHAM! WHAM! I did not have no weapon with me but my purse, but I was going to wham that cop dead in the face with that—when a bottle whammed me on the head. God saved that cop from being slapped with a pocketbook full of knockout punches from poker chips to a bottle of Evening in Paradise, also a big bunch of keys which might of broke his nose.'

" 'Don't you believe in nonviolence?' I asked.

" 'Yes,' said Miss Minnie, 'when the other parties are nonviolent, too. But when I have just come out of a funeral parlor from looking at a little small black boy shot three times by a full-grown cop, I think it is about time I raised my pocketbook and strike at least one blow for freedom. I come up North ten years ago to find freedom, Jesse B. Semple. I did not come to Harlem to look a white army of white cops in the face and let them tell me I can't be free in my own black neighborhood on my own black street in the very year when the Civil Rights Bill says *you shall be free*. No, I didn't! It is a good thing that bottle struck me down, or I would of tore that cop's head every way but loose.'

" 'Then you might not of been here today,' I said.

" 'That is right,' agreed Miss Minnie, 'but my soul would go marching on. Was I to have gone to the morgue instead of Harlem Hospital, I would go crying, "*Freedom now*," and I would come back to haunt them that struck me low. The ghost of Miss Minnie would walk among white folks till their dying day and keep them scared to death. I would incite to riot every week-end in Harlem. I would lead black mobs—which is what the papers said we is—from Friday night to Monday morning. It would cost New York a million dollars a week to just try to keep us Negroes and *me* quiet. They would wonder downtown what got into Harlem. It would just be my spirit egging us on. I would gladly die for freedom and come back to haunt white folks. Yes, I would! Imagine me floating down Lenox Avenue, a white ghost with a blonde wig on!'

" 'I would hate to see you,' I said.

" 'I would hate to see myself,' said Miss Minnie. '*Freedom now!*' She raised her beer glass and I raised mine. Then Miss Minnie said, 'I might not of gave my head to the cause, but I gave my wig.'

"Peoples like to hear Cousin Minnie talk and sometimes when she gets an audience, she goes to town. It being kind of quiet in the bar last night, folks started listening at Minnie instead of playing the juke box, and Minnie proceeded to expostulate on the subject of riots and white and colored leaders advising Harlem to go slow and be cool. Says Minnie, 'When I was down South picking cotton, didn't a soul tell me to go slow and cool it. "Pick more! Pick more! Can't you pick a bale a day? What's wrong with you?" That's what they said. Did not a soul say, "Wait, don't over-pick yourself." Nobody said slow down in cotton-picking days. So what is this here now? When Negroes are trying to get something for themselves, I must wait, *don't demonstrate?* I'll tell them big shots, "How you sound?"

" 'Be cool?' asked Miss Minnie. 'Didn't a soul say, "Be cool," when I was out in that hot sun down South. I heard not nary a word about "be cool." So who is telling me to be cool now? I have not no air cooler in Harlem where I live, neither air conditioner. And you talking about be cool! How you sound?

" 'Get off the streets! Huh! Never did nobody say, 'Get out of the fields,' when I was down home picking cotton in them old cotton fields which I have *not* forgotten. In slavery times, I better not get out of no fields if I wanted to save my hide, or save my belly from meeting my backbone from hunger when freedom came. No! I better stay in them fields and work. But now that I got a street to stand on, how do you sound telling me to get off the street? Just because some little old disturbance come up and a few rocks is throwed in a riot, I am supposed to get off of my street in Harlem and leave it to the polices to rule? I am supposed to go home and be cool? Cool what, where, baby? How do you sound?

" ' "My name is Minnie and I lost my forty-dollar wig in the riots, so I am reduced to my natural hair," I'll tell them leaders. But what is one wig more or less to give for freedom? One wig not to go slow. One wig not to be cool. One wig not to get off the streets. When it is a long hot summer, where else but in the streets, fool, can I be cool? Uncontrollable? Who says I was uncontrollable? Huh! I knowed what I was doing. I did not lose my head because when I throwed a bottle, I knowed what I was throwing at. I were throwing at Jim Crow, Mr. K. K. Krow—at which I aimed my throw. How do you sound, telling me not to aim at Jim Crow?

" 'Did not a soul in slavery time tell old bull-whip marster not to aim his whip at me, at me—a woman. Did not a soul tell that mean old overseer not to hit Harriet Tubman (who is famous every Negro History Week), not to hit her in the head with a rock whilst she was a young girl. She were black, and a slave, and her head was made to be hit with a rock by her white overseer. Did not a soul tell that man who shot Medgar Evers in the back with a bullet to be cool. Did not a soul say to them hoodlums what slayed them three white and colored boys in Mississippi to cool it. Now they calling me hoodlums up here in Harlem for wanting to be free. Hoodlums? Me, a hoodlum? Not a soul said "hoodlums" about them night riders who ride through the South burning black churches and lighting white crosses. Not a soul said "hoodlums" when the bombs went off in Birmingham and blasted four little Sunday School girls to death, little black Sunday School girls. Not a soul said "hoodlums" when they tied an auto rim to Emmett Till's feet and throwed him in that Mississippi river, a kid just fourteen years old. But me, I am a hoodlum when I don't cool it, won't cool it, or lose my wig on a riot gig. They burnt down fourteen colored churches in Mississippi in one summer, yet, I'm supposed to be cool? Even our colored leaders telling Harlem to be cool! Well, I am my own leader, and I am not cool.

" 'Everywhere they herd my people in jail like cattle,

and I am supposed to be cool. I read in one of my colored papers the other day where it has cost Mississippi four million dollars just to keep Negroes in jail. And Savannah, Georgia, spent eighteen thousand in one year feeding black boycotters in jail. One town in North Carolina spent twelve hundred dollars a day on beans for colored students they locked up for marching to be free. One paper said it cost the State of Maryland one hundred thousand dollars a month to send the militia to Cambridge to keep Negroes from getting a cup of coffee in them crumby little old white restaurants which has no decent coffee, nohow, but which everybody ought to have the right to go into on general principles. But me, I can't go in. Yet them that's supposed to be my leaders tell me, 'Give up! Don't demonstrate! Wait!' To tell the truth, I believe my own colored leaders is ashamed of me. So how are they going to lead anybody they are ashamed of? Telling me to be cool. Huh! I'm too hot to be cool—so I guess I will just have to lead my own self—which I dead sure will do. I will lead myself.' "

CONCERNMENT

"The NAACP and the unions is wrestling over color bars in employment," said Simple, "but there is no color bar in unemployment. When a man is unemployed and out of work, be he black or white, his pockets is *equally* empty. A white budget at home with nothing in it is just as budgetless as a black budget with nothing in it. If white wives is like my wife Joyce, when the family budget gets low a husband is liable to be up against some loud talking from his better half. She always claims she could do better if she was a man than her husband can. What makes womens so conceited, do you reckon?"

"I don't know," I said. "Maybe it stems from original sin."

"I know Eve figured she could have had two or three apples, instead of one, if Adam hadn't been so lazy and had gone to the tree and plucked them apples himself, instead of letting that serpent come creeping along with just one little old pippin which is what my old Aunt Lucy, who knowed her Bible, said was the beginning of original sin. And that lone fig leaf Eve wore everywhere she went—Adam could have cut her off enough new fig leaves to make a dress. He didn't. That is one reason Eve fussed at Adam so much."

"How do you know she fussed?" I asked.

"I know women," said Simple. "I bet Eve and Adam fussed and quarreled and hollered, then cussed so much, they should have been named Atom and Evil. Anyhow, if Adam had been out working somewhere, instead of lounging around in the Garden of Eden, he would have got along much better with his wife. Women do not like a man around just doing nothing. I am lucky to be working every day. That is why my wife is so glad to see me when I get home. Unemployment is no good, and it is too bad there is so much around these days.

"Everything is always worse for colored than for white, because we have less to begin with, so if we lose that little bit, where are we at?" asked Simple. "That is why a recession for white folks is a depression for us. But if the NAACP can open up the unions, maybe there will be a few more jobs around, at least."

"A great many more," I said.

"Except of course, if a Negro was ever to drive a train," said Simple, "I mean run a diesel engine on the Florida Express, the government would probably have to put a troop train in front and a troop train behind and B-29s overhead to get that train through Georgia. And the first Negro engineer on a New York-to-Jackson train would have to be protected like Meredith was at Ole Miss. If they also had colored conductors on that train, every coach would have to have soldiers in the vestibules and the FBI in the smoking rooms. It is no great big job for a conductor to collect tickets on a train, so why do you reckon them railroad unions will let a Negro *buy* a ticket but won't let him *collect* one? The railroads will let a Negro ride in a coach, but will not let him run an engine. In New York City, Negroes drive subway trains. They drive trucks. They run busses. Why cannot a Negro also run an American train on an American railroad in this American country?"

"Ha! Ha!" I laughed.

"Because a Negro is a Negro," said Simple. "I am telling you, we has so many problems, life is liable to kill us before death does. In the old days, you did not hear of Negroes committing suicide so much like you do now. Lately, we is getting just like white folks, taking sleeping pills by the handful, drinking poisons, jumping off George Washington bridges, driving Cadillacs into walls on purpose, also turning on gas and breathing our last instead of using that gas to cook dinner with. Crazy peoples are walking around talking to themselves, setting up in the subway muttering and mumbling all to their lonesome selves, whirling and twirling in the middle of the street in front of cars. Such things I did not see in the good old days when I first come to Harlem. Problems is driving colored folks crazy now, too, just like white folks."

"I think, my dear fellow," I said, "it is simply that as one grows older, one is more aware of the woes of the world. In your youth, when you were bright, optimistic, buoyant, self-centered, and young, your eyes were blind. Now you have more discernment."

"More concernment," said Simple, "which is what I wish the unions would have, too, because every man ought to have the right to work. Harlem is too full of hustlers these days. Fact is, in the opinion of some people I know who would like to be hipsters," said Simple, "work is the last refuge of a square, but hustling is an honorable hype."

"With which I totally disagree," I said. "Work saves the human race from sin, boredom, stagnation, and running amuck. Without work, what would you do with your day?"

"Waste it away," said Simple. "I could waste without haste. I could find plenty of ways to occupy my time, if I was not working. But I am not constituted to hustle."

"That I believe," I said. "You are no hypster. In fact, you cannot even lie with a straight face. But you certainly can con your friends out of beers. At this very bar, how many times have I treated you to drinks without any recompense whatsoever?"

"You know, me and Joyce have to balance our budget, and my wife does not count in beers," said Simple.

"I have to balance my budget, too," I said.

"Yes," said Simple, "but a woman balances different from a man. You are not married so, whenever you want to, you can shift your balance around—and pull a hype on yourself. But my wife wants our budget to come out even each and every week. A woman's voice is sweet to hear when it is full of love, but not when the budget don't balance. Joyce can figure backwards, count pennies down to the last Indian head, and don't mess with dollar bills! Every time I break a dollar, I think about what will happen at home. When I was a single man, I didn't care whichaway or where my dollars went."

"But your landlady did," I said. "I recall many a time you had to borrow from me to pay your rent."

"Bring up not such unpleasant subjects," said Simple. "That were far away and long ago. My wife keeps me and the landlord straight now. But, at least, I *borrowed* from you. I did not beg, neither steal, con, nor hype anybody out of a cent. I would not even take money from Zarita, who loved me, even if we had no legal ties. But, to be a decent bar girl, Zarita could lay down plenty of hypes herself—and still does, I reckon, wherever she may be. Zarita and my Cousin Minnie both knew how to get the ups on a man without giving in to him. Many a poor joker has sacrificed his week's wages to them womens just for a smile. Zarita was pretty, anyhow, but Minnie looks like come-what-may and worse today. Still and yet, that cousin of mine has got something that glues a man to a bar stool, if he is setting next to her. Without being a hustler, Minnie is one of the best lady hypsters since Eve hyped Adam. Some people, male or either female, just naturally have talent for laying down a hype. I don't, which is probably why I do not bother."

"You have a conscience," I said, "which in our day and time not everyone is born with. The typical hypster is what the psychology books term amoral, if not actually immoral—unconscious of sin, really, even though a sinner."

"I wish I could be unconscious of my budget," said Simple. "Say, brother—"

"I did not know we were related," I said, sensing what was coming.

"Well then, *friend*—listen," said Simple. "Before you embarrassed me, I was going to ask you another favor—as of old. Lend me a five."

"Until when?" I asked. "May Day, when you *may* pay?"

"Why be technical?" said Simple. "But if you did lend me a five, I was going to treat *you* to a beer."

"On such a rare occasion, I cannot resist," I said. "Here!"

"Bartender," cried Simple, "a beer—one for me and one for this unbudgeted steer! And now to get back on the subject of hypers, hypsters, and hustling. You know, peoples hustles in a lot of different ways. Some sell their bodies and some sell their souls. My feeling is, if you are gonna sell either, try to get a good price."

"Some people simply sell honest labor," I said.

"Yes, but they usually don't get anywhere," declared Simple lifting his beer. "The ones that has the fine houses and the fine cars and drinks the best whiskey is most in generally them that sells their souls. A few makes it to the upper brackets with their bodies—but they is mostly womens with the right telephone numbers."

"You mean, I suppose, kept women and call girls," I said, "because the poor bar-stool hustlers and street-walkers wouldn't be in bars and on corners if they made anything."

"I am also talking about womens who marry money *for money*," said Simple, looking at his already empty glass on the bar. "But marrying money happens to very few colored womens. There are not enough colored men around with fortunes for many of our womens to make them their targets. Of course, a few colored folks in show business marry whites. But it is the colored celebrities that usually has the money, my wife says, and the whites marry them to get it."

"I think your wife is making a completely unjustified statement," I said. "A celebrity, white or colored, may marry for love just like anybody else."

"It is not necessary to marry to get love," said Simple, "so why confuse the issue? I am not opposed to intermarriage myself. But my wife, Joyce, blows her top at the very mention of it. Joyce says if we had a son what married white, she would put him out of the house.

"I said, 'Joyce, baby, he probably would not want to live in Harlem, nohow.'

"Joyce said, 'Let him go down to the Village then and live in sin.'

" 'What do you mean,' I asked her, 'live in sin, if they've got a marriage license?'

" 'To me,' said Joyce, 'it is living in sin for a colored man to marry anybody related to Talmadge, Eastland, Wallace, Sheriff Clark, and Satan—and all white folks bears kinship.'

"I did not argue with Joyce, because when she gets on that subject, we will not be moved. When my wife has a point, she likes to gnaw at it like a dog with a bone. When Joyce sees a mixed couple on the street, that gives her a point. It is one of her main concernments. But me, I do not understand how my wife can work for integration, give money to CORE, the NAACP, and all, yet get mad when she sees integration in action. Colored womens can be a contradiction. Am I right or wrong?"

"All women are contradictions," I said. "But contradictions are a part of their charm. 'Inconsistency, thy name is woman,' I quote. Or maybe it's 'inconstancy.' "

"Boyd, your diploma is worth every penny you paid for it," said Simple. "Only a man who is colleged could talk like that. Me, I speaks simpler, myself."

"Simplicity can sometimes be more devious than erudition," I said, "especially when it centers in an argumentative ego like yours."

"Of course," said Simple.

STATUTES AND STATUES

"There were so many policemens uptown the week Malcolm X was buried that Harlem looked like a Cops Convention. And down in Selma, Alabama, that week the polices were so busy arresting Negroes that they had to swear in extra officers recruited from the Ku Klux Klan," said Simple. "It must have cost the City of New York a half million dollars to keep all them policemens up in Harlem all week long, what with overtime and all. And the State of Alabam' is almost gone broke arresting Negroes and feeding them in jail. It looks to me like it would be cheaper for white folks just to go ahead and give Negroes whatever it is they want, and stop having to spend so much money on polices, and jail bills, and court cases, and fat old judges making decrees that nobody pays any attention to. All this costs so much money!"

"Yes, it does," I said.

"But then the white folks have all the money," said Simple, "so they probably do not mind spending it. There is always more for them where that came from. But for Negroes the hardest thing is to try to get just three or four hundred dollars ahead. A black man has hardly got enough money to even get from Brooklyn to the Bronx, let alone a little extra change for a stopover in Harlem. We are a *broke* race of people. That is why I am all for trying to collect what is owed my great grandpa and grandma from slavery days for all that free labor my ancestries did in this American country!"

"The statute of limitations has long since passed," I said.

"Maybe that is why them dynamiters wanted to blow up that statue," said Simple.

"I am not talking about the Statue of Liberty," I said. "I am speaking of *limitations*."

"Which is about all we got," said Simple, "because the Statue of Liberty has her back turned toward Harlem."

"Liberty has always been looking out to sea," I said, "whence came the white Americans. But Africans arrived via the southern routes, mostly landing in Virginia and the Carolinas and places like that—long before Liberty lit her torch."

"Only Ku Klux Klan torches blazing," said Simple. "You know, as long as I have been in Harlem, I have not yet looked Liberty in the face, but I know she is beautiful on the postcards. And I hope she don't get blowed up before I see what she looks like. Where do you reckon folks is getting all these bombs and dynamite to blow things up these days when a child can't even buy a firecracker just for fun at Fourth of July time? Firecrackers is against the law. But it looks like almost anybody can get a stick of dynamite, a small bomb, a rifle, or a pistol if they want to do something wrong. But good people like me better not be caught by the polices with no kind of weapon, not even for protection in a self-service elevator.

"What can I carry to guard against the junkies who need thirty dollars for a fix? Junkies should be able to tell by looking at me that I do not have any money. But a junkie in need will steal even the widow's mite. The city ought to start a Junk Fund to take care of poor junkies and pay for their fixes, so they don't have to rob old ladies and stick up cabbies. The city used to have free Soup Stands during the Depression, so the city ought to set up free Junk Stands now."

"The English system amounts, in effect, to about what you are saying. Over there they have Dope Depots to supply the addict with his daily needs. Such a setup in New York could cut the rug out from under the heroin pushers and the big boys who make the million-dollar profits. Free Junk Stands would cut crime in half."

"I agree," said Simple, "because then the junkies would not have to rob *me* to pay the pushers. So let the city stop spending so much money on cops to keep the ordinary Negroes in line, and spend some bread on free dope to keep the junkies in line. I think it is worse for a junkie to beat and rob an old woman in Queens than it is for a Negro to start a riot in Harlem. Them that participates in riots are usually big enough and ugly enough to take care of themselves. But an old lady of eighty-three, no. Or a lone man or lone woman caught in a self-service elevator by herself, no! Push-button elevators was made for stick-ups. There has not been an elevator man in most elevators in Harlem for years. The junkies *love* the elevator in our building. When a crazy junkie gets on at the second floor, what can you do? Or suppose you are a taxi driver in that front seat by his lonesome self in a lonesome neighbor-hood—and the guys in the back seat are desperate for dope money! I say let the city put into its new budget a big appropriation for Free Junk Stands—and give dope away."

"Your suggestion would be ridiculed at City Hall," I said.

"Maybe not by that new Borough President we got," said Simple. "That woman is good-looking and smart, too."

"Mrs. Motley is a handsome woman," I said.

"She looks like the Statue of Liberty to me," said Simple. "And her back is not turned to Harlem, because she lived in Harlem, and she knows what I am talking about. She knows we have got one million cops and a half million junkies and we need some free dope."

"Your figures are extremely in error," I said. "Besides you are confusing the issues."

"The issues are confusing me," said Simple. "But I hope that nice Motley lady does not live in a house with a self-service elevator. If she does, the city ought to take one of them parlays of cops off of one of our Harlem corners and give them to her for protection at night when she comes home from City Hall. With so many junkies around eying push-button elevators needing thirty-dollar-a-day fixes, I do not want anything to happen to my Statue of Liberty."

"You mean Constance Baker Motley?"

"I do," said Simple.

AMERICAN DILEMMA

"When I come around the corner last night here in Harlem," said Simple, "and nearly run into a white cop strolling around the corner from the other way, I almost said, 'Birmingham.'"

"Almost? What did you say instead?" I asked.

"Nothing," said Simple.

"What did the cop say?"

"Nothing, neither," said Simple. "If he had been a colored cop and I had bumped into him, I would have said, 'Excuse me.' But he being white, I did not say nothing. And what I thought was Birmingham."

"Seemingly then, you equate all white people with the brutalities of Birmingham, even whites in New York."

"I do," said Simple. "After dark, Harlem is black, except for cops. Here of lately, it looks like there is more white cops than ever strolling around our corners at night. They must be expecting more trouble."

"What 'they'?" I asked.

"The white folks downtown. If there was as many black cops downtown in New York as there is white cops uptown in Harlem, you would know something was wrong. I reckon it is Alabama and Mississippi making the white folks downtown afraid Harlem might get mad again and start breaking up things, like they did in the riots."

"I admit there is often tension in the air," I said. "But do you think it will reach riot proportions again?"

"All I know is, when I come around that corner last night off Lenox Avenue and run into that white cop, when he saw me he looked like he was scared. You know I am no dangerous man. I am what folks calls an ordinary citizen. Me, I work, pay my rent, and taxes, and try to get along. But that young white cop looked at me like he were afraid of me. I do not much blame him, up here in Harlem all by hisself at midnight A.M. in the middle of Negroes. Lenox Avenue can get real lonesome-looking late at night. When I saw that cop and thought about Birmingham, I bet he saw me and thought about riots.

"He were a young cop. Maybe he just recently got on the force. Maybe he needs to earn some steady money to take care of his wife and kids and buy hisself a house in some neighborhood where there is no Negroes. None of these white cops here in Harlem ever live in Harlem. They say Harlem is the place where the Police Department puts rookies and green young cops to break them in. Or else they put old cops who has done wrong in some other part of New York, maybe taken graft that should have gone to the precinct captain, or something like that. So they put them up in Harlem for a punishment. Anyhow, the other night, here is this young white cop coming around the corner, and here is me coming around the corner. We almost bump. I pass, he passes, and nobody says nothing.

"In a way, I felt sorry for that young white cop. Was I not colored and he not white, I would have said, 'Good evening! It's kind of quiet tonight, ain't it?' And maybe he would have said, 'Good evening,' back. But neither one of us said nothing. I almost bumped into him. He almost bumped into me, curving that corner, and nobody even said, 'Good evening,' let alone, 'Excuse me.' All I thought about was Birmingham. What he thought I do not know."

"I gather then that there was no friendly word exchanged between you—you, citizen, and he, policeman, guardian of the law."

"No friendly word," said Simple.

PROMULGATIONS

"If I was setting in the High Court in Washington," said Simple, "where they do not give out no sentences for crimes, but where they gives out promulgations, I would promulgate. Up them long white steps behind them tall white pillars in that great big marble hall with the eagle of the U.S.A., where at I would bang my gavel and promulgate."

"Promulgate what?" I asked.

"Laws," said Simple. "After that I would promulgate the promulgations that would take place if people did not obey my laws. I see no sense in passing laws if nobody pays them any mind."

"What would happen if people did not obey your promulgations?" I asked.

"Woe be unto them," said Simple. "I would not be setting in that High Court paid a big salary just to read something off a paper. I would be there with a robe on to see that what I read was carried out. I would gird on my sword, like in the Bible, and prepare to do battle. For instant, 'Love thy neighbor as thyself.' The first man I caught who did not love his neighbor as hisself, I would make him change places with his neighbor—the rich with the poor, the white with the black, and Governor Faubus with me."

"I know you have lost your mind," I said. "How could you accomplish such an objective?"

"With education," said Simple, "which white folks favors. I would make Governor Faubus go to school again in Little Rock and study with them integrated students there and learn all over again the facts of life."

"You are telling me *what* you would do," I said, "not *how* you would do it. How could you make Faubus do anything?"

"I would say, 'Faubus! Faubus! Come out of that clothes closet or wherever you are hiding and face me. *Me*, Jesse B., who has promulgated your attendance in my presence! I decrees now and from here on out that you straighten up and fly right. Cast off your mask of ignorance and hate and go study your history. You have not yet learned that "taxation without representation is tyranny," which I learned in grade school. You have also not learned that "all men are created equal," which I learned before I quit school. Educate yourself, Faubus, so that you can better rule your state.' "

"Suppose he paid you no attention?" I said.

"Then I would whisper something in his ear," said Simple. "I would tell him that the secret records in the hands of my committee show that he has got colored blood. Whilst he was trying to recover from that shock, I would continue with some facts I made up.

" 'Governor Faubus, did you not know your great-great-grandfather were black?'

"He would say, 'What?'

"I would say, 'Look at me, Governor, I am your third cousin.' Whereupon Faubus would faint. Whilst he was fainted, I would pick him up and take him to a mixed school. When he come to, he would be integrated. That is the way I would work my promulgations," said Simple.

"I should think you would rapidly become a national figure," I said, "with your picture in *Time*, *Life*, *Newsweek*, *Ebony*, and *Jet*."

"Yes," said Simple. "Then in my spare time I would take up the international situation. I would call a Summit Meeting and get together with all the big heads of state in the world."

"I gather you would drop your judgeship for the nonce and become a diplomat."

"A hip-to-mat," said Simple, "minding everybody's business but my own. I would call my valet to tell my confidential secretary to inform my aide to bring me my attaché case. I would put on my swallowtail coat, striped trousers, and high hat, get into my limousine, and ride to the Summit looking like an Englishman. But what would be different about me is I would be black. I would take my black face, black hands, and black demands right up to the top and set down and say, 'Gimme a microphone, turn on the TVs, and hook up the national hookups. I want the world to hear my message.' Then I would promulgate at large as I proceeded to chair the agenda."

"Proceed," I said.

"Which I would do," said Simple, "no sooner than the audience got settled, the diplomats got their earphones strapped on, and the translators got their dictionaries out, also the stenographers got their machines ready to take my message from Harlem down for the record. The press galleries would be full of reporters waiting to wire my words around the world, and I would be prepared to send them, Jack. I would be ready."

"Give forth," I said.

"Bread and meat come first," said Simple. " 'Gentlemens of the Summit, I want you-all to think how you can provide everybody in the world with bread and meat. Civil rights comes next. Let everybody have civil rights, white, black, yellow, brown, gray, grizzle, or green. No Jim-Crow-take-low can't go for anybody! Let Arabs go to Israel and Israels go to Egypt, Chinese come to America and Negroes live in Australia, if any be so foolish as to want to. Let Willie Mays live in Levittown and Casey Stengel live in Ghana if he so desires. And let me drink at the Stork Club if I get tired of Small's Paradise. Open house before open skies. After which comes peace, which you can't have nohow as long as peoples and nations is snatching and grabbing over pork chops and payola so as not to starve to death. No peace could be had nohow with white nations against dark.

" 'You big countries of the world has got to wake up to the sense your leaders wasn't born with, and the peoples has got to reach out their hands to each others' over the leaders' heads, just like I am talking over your leaders' heads now, because so many leaders is in the game for payola and say-ola, not *do*-ola. But me, self-appointed, I am beholden to nobody. Right now I can do much, but I can say *all*.

" 'I therefore say to you, gentlemens of the Summit, you may not pay attention to me now, but some sweet day you will. I will get tired of your stuff and your bluff. I will take your own golf stick and wham the world so far up into orbit until you will be shaken off the surface of the earth and everybody will wonder where have all the white folks gone. Gentlemens of the Summit, you-all had better get together and straighten up and fly right—else in due time you will have to contend with what Harlem thinks. Do I hear some of you-all say, "It do not matter what Harlem thinks"?

"'I regret to inform you, gentlemens of the Summit, that IT DO!'"

HOW OLD IS OLD?

"I looked in the mirror today and I saw my first gray hair," said Simple, "this morning."

"That's nothing," I said. "Some morning you will look in your mirror and see several gray hairs."

"Sometime I might look in the mirror and see *all* gray hairs," said Simple, "but I will not like it. The chicks will say I am old."

"Gray hair does not necessarily make a man old," I said. "Some folks become gray at quite an early age, others bald."

"I had rather be gray-headed than bald-headed," said Simple. "I never did want to look like Yul Brynner."

"Yul Brynner probably shaves his hair off."

"I want neither a razor nor nature nor tomorrow to take what little hair I own. Neither do I want to look like Uncle Mose before my time. I pulled out that gray hair I spotted in my head this morning."

"Little did I think you would be so vain, partner."

"Little did I think I was getting so old," said Simple. "But come right down to it, I have been in this world quite a while. I survived being born, being a child, being a man, and being married twice. I have also survived being an Afro-American, colored, and a so-called Negro.

"I have survived bad feet, a bad head the morning after, bad weather, and a bad back, also checks that bounce, landladies that bark, bite, and bifferate, plus a wife, Isabel, who did not understand me in my youthhood, neither I understood her.

"Oh, I have stood much in this world that I did not understand, and standed much that I did not understood, also undergone mistreatment from one billion white folks, one million colored folks, one hundred bosses, and one bartender who would not let me have a beer on credit.

"I have spent so much money in that place up the street that I ought to own that beer bar. I said to the barman up there last night, 'How come you come telling me the state liquor laws do not allow you to grant a customer credit? Why do them laws discriminate against me? You, the bartender, drink as much as you want to when the boss is not looking and do not pay a dime, not even credit. How come I cannot drink as much as I want and pay on time in *due* time?'

" 'It is the law of the License Commission,' says the bartender.

" 'Then you gimme one of them free drinks I see you sneaking into your mouth. I will sneak some change into your hand when I get paid.'

" 'Against the law,' says the bartender.

" 'Then treat me,' I says.

" 'Also illegal,' says the bartender. 'My boss does not budget no treats.'

" 'Then I will budget myself to another bar down the street,' says I, which I did, which is why I am in this new bar tonight and you could not find me until I hailed you passing by the window. Being my friend, unmarried, and without a budget, buy me a beer."

"I thought you were working around to something," I said. "O.K., since you are hard-up tonight—one beer for this gentleman, bartender!"

"Maybe two," said Simple, "because I still wish to argue with you on this subject of old age. How old is a man before he gets to be an old man? Forty, fifty, or sixty? Seventy-five I know is ageable, but am I old? I only been married twice."

WEIGHT IN GOLD

"Like Billy Eckstine and Frank Sinatra's son, I wish I was rich enough to be kidnapped," said Simple, "because if I was, I would have done spent all my money before the kidnapping happened. I would never let them hold me for ransom, because the ransom money would be gone. I would just say, 'Boys, you have come too late. My pockets and my bank account is both now turned inside out. I have run through my million. Better to have had and spent than never to have had at all.'"

"My dear fellow," I countered, "if you ever possessed a great deal of money, say a million or so, you would find it next to impossible to spend it all. Besides, if you were sensible, you would invest the principal and live on the interest, like most rich people do."

"I would not be sensible," said Simple. "If I had money, I would go stark-raving mad and spend it! I could not stand being rich. There is so much I have wanted in past days, and so much I still want now—I would just spend it all, yes. And what I did not spend, I would give away to peoples I love. I would give Joyce, my wife, one hundred thousand dollars. I would look up Zarita, that old gal of mine, and, for old times' sake, I would give her fifty thousand dollars. To you, Boyd, my old beer buddy, I would give twenty-five thousand, and to my Cousin

Minnie, ten, so she would not have to borrow from me any more. Also, I would present Minnie with a brand-new wig, since she lost hers in the riots. And for every neighbor kid I know, I would buy a bicycle, because I think every boy—and girl, too, if they wants—should have a bicycle while young."

"In this New York traffic, as heavy as it is, you would give kids bicycles?"

"They can always ride in Central Park," said Simple. "When I were a kid, I always wanted a bicycle, and nobody ever bought me one. To tell the truth, if I was rich I would buy myself a bicycle right now. Then next month I would buy me a motorcycle. I always wanted one of them to make noise on. Then after riding around on my motorcycle for a couple of weeks, I would buy me a small car, just big enough for me and Joyce. After which I would buy a *big* car, then a Town and Country, then a station wagon. After that I would get a foreign sports car. I would do this gradual, not letting the world know all at once that I am rich. Also, I would not like to be kidnapped until *all* the money were spent. I would like to have my fun first, then be kidnapped with my name in the papers. 'JESSE B. SEMPLE NABBED BY MOB. *Held For Ransom. Harlem Shaken by the News.*'"

"You would be missed in this bar," I said.

"If I was rich, I would own this bar," said Simple. "I would buy up all the bars in Harlem and keep the present white proprietors employed as managers. I would not draw no color line. Of course, if the white mens quit and did not want to work under me, black, I would go to HARYOU and ask them to send me some bright young colored managers."

"HARYOU?" I said. "HARYOU hardly supplies bartenders, does it?"

"I would not request bartenders," said Simple. "I would be employing colored *managers*. They tell me HARYOU is set up to give young Negroes a chance."

"Why, tell me, please, if you had money," I asked, "would you buy only bars? Why not restaurants, grocery stores, clothing shops, wiggeries?"

"Because bars has the quickest turnover," said Simple. "Besides, if I owned all the Harlem bars, I would have credit in each and every one of them. I would never have to ask anybody to buy me a beer. In fact, I would treat *you* every time we met. Oh, if I was rich, daddy-o, I would be a generous son-of-a-gun, specially with everybody I like. I not only like you, Boyd, but I admire you. You are colleged. You know, if I had money, I would send every young man and young woman in Harlem to college, that wanted to go. I would set up one of these offices that gives out money for education."

"You mean a Foundation for Fellowships," I said.

"And Girlships, too," declared Simple. "Womens and mens from Harlem would all be colleged by the time 1970 came. It do not take but four years to get colleged, do it?"

"That's right," I said, "depending on your application."

"I would tell all the boys and girls in Harlem to make their applications now," said Simple, "and I would see that they got through. White folks downtown would have no excuse any more to say we was not educated uptown, because I would pay for it."

"In other words, you would be Harlem's Ford Foundation," I said, "on a really big scale."

"Yes," said Simple, "because on my scales, every kid in Harlem is worth his weight in gold."

SYMPATHY

"Some people do not have no scars on their faces," said Simple, "but they has scars on their hearts. Some people have never been beat up, teeth knocked out, nose broke, shot, cut, not even so much as scratched in the face. But they have had their hearts broke, brains disturbed, their minds torn up, and the behinds of their souls kicked by the ones they love. It is not always your wife, husband, sweetheart, boy friend or girl friend, common-law mate—no, it might be your mother that kicks your soul around like a football. It might be your best friend that squeezes your heart dry like a lemon. It might be some ungrateful child you have looked forward to making something out of when it got grown, but who goes to the dogs and bites you on the way there. Oh, friend, your heart can be scarred in so many different ways it is not funny," said Simple.

"Why do you bring up such unpleasant subjects on a pleasant evening?" I asked. "We have got two nice cold glasses of beer sitting up here in front of us at the bar, and we could be talking about President Johnson and his budget problems."

"Or about Adam Powell and the lady they say he called an old bag-woman," said Simple.

"Or about who kidnapped Billy Eckstine and took the ransom out of his own pocket," I added.

"Else why Cassius Clay stuck by Elijah Muhammad instead of Malcolm X."

"Or why Malcolm X changed his name to el-Hajj Malik Shabazz."

"Or how come, if you are a Black Muslim, a man can change his name any time he wants to," said Simple.

"We could even be talking about the weather," I said.

"Or the price of eggs," agreed Simple. "But I am talking about how a man's heart or a woman's *is not* an egg, and, broken though your heart may be, it is seldom busted. It is a good thing folks cannot crack the heart and drop the insides in a frying pan like an egg. It is a good thing a man cannot make an omelette out of your trouble. Your ticker may be battered, mistreat it as you might, but that old heart keeps on beating until you die *d-e-a-d* dead."

"Who did what to your heart, old man, that you keep on harping on the same subject this evening? Did your wife look at you cross-eyed when you came home from work tonight? Is Joyce on the rampage?"

"No," said Simple. "My subject has nothing to do with myself. I am standing here thinking about Cousin Minnie. In spite of her faults, Minnie is a good woman, although somewhat overweight, and inclined to borrow money from her relatives when she ought to get out and earn it herself. Last year, you know, Cousin Minnie thought she had found a good man who would neither beat her nor cheat her, kick or mistreat her, and would never go upside her head. This man did not do such heavy-handed things. But he did worse. Hainsworth lived a lie in Minnie's presence. He kept another woman around the corner with who he spent half the night. When Hainsworth come home to Minnie, it were almost time to get up and go to work. But this was not so bad. He told this other woman things on Minnie that a man should not tell God. He talked about Minnie like a dog outside the home, and this is what hurted Minnie the most—that this other woman should know more about her than she knowed about herself—and from Hainsworth."

"How did Minnie find out all this?" I asked.

"At the beauty shop," said Simple, "which is where womens exchange news, regardless of who is listening over the partitions. In Harlem the beauty shop booths is so close together, anybody is liable to hear anything. And Minnie overheard it from the horse's mouth—the other woman's—direct, herself—even as to what kind of skin lightener Minnie uses before she goes to bed. Also that Minnie has a strawberry birthmark on her left-hand thigh —which nobody could know to tell anybody except Hainsworth."

"I'll be dogged!" I said.

"Yes," said Simple, "that is what broke Minnie's heart."

"Temporarily, I hope."

"Minnie will recover," said Simple.

"Such little things," I said, "should hardly break a woman's heart."

"A small pin can puncture a big balloon," stated Simple. "Minnie's pride were like a big balloon and her love for Hainsworth were great—until she found out he had told this other woman all them things. She said to the whole beauty shop that Minnie could not even boil rice proper, neither fry fish crisp, that she made soggy bisquits and bitter coffee, and also Minnie looked like a pig in a poke when she come to bed."

"Great day!" I exclaimed. "What did Minnie say to Hainsworth?"

"She hit him in the head with a small hammer," said Simple.

"What? Where is he now?"

"In Harlem Hospital with a knot on his noggin like a hen's egg, also a split over his left eye which dead sure will leave a scar. But Minnie has a scar on her heart—which is worse," said Simple. "Also Minnie has lost her faith in men, plus losing her meal ticket. Hainsworth were a good provider. Only trouble was, he were feeding two womens. Now both of them will suffer with him off the job. Had not that other girl blabbed so much in that beauty shop, both of them womens could have had a good dinner tonight."

"That's a shame," I said.

"Yes, it is a shame," said Simple. "To have a scar on your heart is bad enough, but to have nothing in your stomach is worse."

"That's bad," I agreed.

"Yes," affirmed Simple. "That *is* bad, especially since lately Minnie has not been feeling well. Do you know what she told me last night? Out of the clear blue sky in this bar Minnie said, 'Jess, the doctors say I have a tumor, and when they say that, you are liable to have cancer,' said Miss Minnie. 'I am going to the hospital on Monday, Jess Semple. Good-by.'

" 'Just like that, you say good-by tonight? And you are going home this early?'

" 'Yes,' said Miss Minnie. 'I did not tell you I was sick before, I do not tell you I am sick now. But I am. Monday I go to be prepared for the operation. Maybe it might not take like vaccination. If it do not take, I am gone to Glory.

If I go to Glory, maybe you will remember me who set beside you once on this bar stool. And if not, or if so, anyhow, good-by.'

" 'Cousin, are you sure enough really sick? Are you telling me straight?'

" 'Yes, straight—and it's late. Good-by.'

" 'Late what?'

" 'Just late, that's all. Good-by.' And she left."

"She left?"

"Yes."

"Just like that?"

"Just like that. Minnie did not even tell me what hospital she would be in—Harlem, Bellevue, Medical Center, or where. She just left. Minnie would borrow money from me at the drop of a hat. Yes, she would. But I guess she don't want to borrow sympathy."

"No?"

"No," said Simple, "I guess she don't. She just up and left."

UNCLE SAM

"Nobody is responsible for the relatives you is born with," said Simple. "You are only responsible for them which you yourself have taken unto yourself of your own free will. I have taken unto myself Joyce, my wife, and I love her. But I was born related to Minnie, that off-cousin who latched onto me since she come up North. Yet and still, God knows why, somehow I love her, although she can be a nuisance. Maybe because Cousin Minnie takes for granted she understands me, which I do her."

"By and large, you have the same interests," I said.

"By and large, we do," said Simple. "We both likes stools when they are in front of bars. Anyhow, after all, she is a relative, even though on the off-side, and I am sorry she is sick. My Uncle Sam is on the off-side, too. But I have never met Uncle Sam in the flesh."

"I did not know you had an uncle named Sam," I said.

"I have. You have, too. But we are not responsible for him. I am talking about the old man in the tight pants, the swallowtail coat, and the star-spangled hat who lives in the attic above the President at the top of the White House. Uncle Sam must have lost his wife, because I never hear of an Auntie Sam. Else he never married. But they say he is my uncle."

"On which side of the family?" I asked. "Your mother's?"

"Don't slip me in the dozens," said Simple, "or I will tell you on which side you are related yourself. There would have to be some crossbreeding somewhere. I am talking about the MAN, the American Man, the one with the pointed goatee. I mean the MAN on all the recruiting posters: UNCLE SAM WANTS YOU, pointing dead at me. When I was young enough to be drafted, Uncle Sam used to scare me half to death. But even then I had some questions for him. I said, 'Uncle Sam, if you is really my blood uncle, prove it. Before you draft me into any United States Army, prove your kinship. Are we *is*, or are we *ain't* related? If so, how come you are so white and I am so dark? Uncle Sam, explain myself.' "

"Did he ever answer you?" I asked.

"No," said Simple, "that is why I want to know if Uncle Sam *is* or *ain't*. He knows I am colored."

"So?"

"He is white."

"So?"

"So therefore Uncle Sam do not have to sue in the Supreme Court every time he wants to get a cup of coffee down South," said Simple. "Neither do Uncle Sam have to sue in Mississippi every time he wants to vote."

"Segregation will end and the ballot will come in due time," I said.

"So will death," said Simple.

"The Constitution, the government, the law are now all on the Negro's side."

"But is Uncle Sam?" asked Simple.

"As a symbol of the government, I would say *yes*—looking back, yes, Roosevelt, Kennedy, and today Johnson."

"Faubus, Barnett, Eastland," said Simple.

"I am not kidding." I frowned.

"Me, neither," said Simple. "They make a lot of star-spangled hats in Washington. I wants one for me."

"Why?"

"So I can be Uncle Sam," said Simple.

"You sound like Nipsey Russell. Fact is, with a star-spangled hat on, you would look like Nipsey."

"Nipsey I like on TV," said Simple, "so I could bear the resemblance. The government ought to make some great big subway posters of Nipsey as Uncle Sam. I say, there ought to be a *black* Uncle Sam."

"Chauvinist!" I said.

"If that word means what I think it do," cried Simple, "take it back."

"It does not mean that," I said, "so continue."

"What does it mean?" asked Simple.

"A man who is so full of racism that nobody else can stand him. Or another definition might be somebody like yourself who wants to make Uncle Sam black."

"Or at least brownskin," said Simple. "Or maybe Indian like the original Americans, or Chinese like Chinese-Americans, or Japanese like them Niseis in California. Since it is popular to integrate nowadays, how come Uncle Sam is never pictured as if maybe his mama had integrated before him?"

"Do you know what you are saying?" I asked. "You are speaking of miscegenation, not integration. The Uncle Sam you see on the signboards is, of course, of Nordic descent."

"I am tired of seeing my Uncle always of Nordic descent," said Simple. "I want to see him look like me—colored for once."

"Uncle Sam is a symbol, as I said. He is not meant to be of any one race or group. Symbols have no color."

"Then I want him to be a symbol of *me* once," said Simple. "I have never yet seen an Uncle Sam that looked like me."

"You seem to dwell in a world of fantasy," I said. "Suppose tomorrow all the newspapers were to picture Uncle Sam as colored, could you believe your eyes?"

"If I saw myself, *yes*. Adam Clayton Powell would also make a good-looking Uncle Sam," said Simple. "Or for a young version, Harry Belafonte would be handsome. But Sidney Poitier would be the stone-most! Star-spangled Uncle Sam! Or let's take Miss America with a sheet draped around her, looking like the Statue of Liberty. I have never yet seen her colored. If I was an artist, I would sometimes draw America looking like Marian Anderson, or Claudia McNeil who was in *Raisin in the Sun*. I do not see why Claudia would not make a knockout Miss America, full-bosomed as she is."

"Dream on," I said.

"Well, at least, they could make Miss America a Red Indian," said Simple. "Indians was the first Americans, but they got pushed back so much by the cowboys in the movies until now they is the *last* Americans. But in honor of the fact that they was once the first, there ought to be Indian Uncle Sams, too, and Indian Miss Americas."

"At least, their heads were once on a penny," I said.

"But no Negroes," said Simple. "Our heads have never even been on a penny. Neither on a dollar bill, nor on a five-dollar bill, nor a ten. And I have not seen a Negro on a postage stamp since Booker T. Washington."

"Frederick Douglass is lately on a stamp," I said. "However, Negroes are only about ten percent of the American population."

"But we raise ninety percent of the hell," said Simple, "so I want to see a Freedom Rider on a postage stamp, or else Martin Luther King, or me dressed like Uncle Sam. We have been mighty near one hundred years free. It is not easy by and large to live one hundred years in the Land of the Free, if black you be—so I deserves my head on a stamp."

"What kind of stamp?" I asked.

"The first space-stamp," said Simple, "designed to fly off into orbit—out of this world. Free! Uncle Sam *me*—on a letter to the moon!"

"Dream on, dreamer," I said, "dream on."